It's a Beautiful Day
Life's Outtakes - Year 13

52 Humorous and Inspirational Short Stories

By
Daris Howard

A collection of stories, humorous anecdotes, thoughts, and tidbits of wisdom from the newspaper column *Life's Outtakes*.

Publishing Inspiration

It's a Beautiful Day

Life's Outtakes - Year 13

52 Humorous and Inspirational Short Stories

By

Daris W. Howard

A collection of stories, humorous anecdotes, thoughts, and tidbits of wisdom from the newspaper column *Life's Outtakes*.

ISBN-10: 1-62986-023-9
ISBN-13: 978-1-62986-023-7

www.publishinginspiration.com

Publishing Date: January 16, 2020

Publishing Inspiration LLC

Table of Contents

Dear reader,

     People often ask me if my stories are true. Though I must admit that I tend to take a bit of literary license in my writing, each story is based on an actual event. Sometimes the stranger stories are the ones that are stretched the least. As people often say, truth is stranger than fiction.

     I also want to note that some of the names have been changed to protect the anonymity of the individuals.

Daris Howard

A Father's Day Mystery

    Cindy excitedly came into the sewing room where her mother was busy mending overalls. "Mom, guess what I got Dad for Father's Day!"

    Janet looked up from her sewing and smiled. "My guess would be some new tool, probably a hammer."

    "Oh, Mom," Cindy said. "You have no imagination."

    "Maybe not," Janet said. "But I do know your father. And that's what he always requests for Father's Day."

    "You can get him a hammer," Cindy replied. "I decided to be more creative. I got him some cologne."

    Janet smiled. "Cologne. Really? I have bought your father cologne countless times, and do you know how many times he has worn it? A big fat zero, as far as I know. I have never smelled cologne on him once, and the cologne just mysteriously disappears. I figure he just pours it down the drain when I'm not looking."

    "But I have one advantage you don't have," Cindy said.

    "And just what would that be?"

    "I'm his favorite daughter."

    "You only think that because you're the youngest and the only one still at home, so he dotes on you a little bit too much," Janet replied.

    "Nonetheless, I think he will wear cologne if it is a gift from me," Cindy said.

    Janet shrugged. "If you can get your father to wear cologne, you'll be a miracle worker. But you definitely have my blessing to try."

Janet helped Cindy find the perfect wrapping paper for the gift. When Father's Day came, Cindy could hardly wait for her father to open it. When he did, his enthusiasm and gratitude seemed boundless.

"Do you like it?" Cindy asked.

"I love this stuff," her father replied. "It is wonderful."

Cindy whispered an "I told you so" to her mother, who, in turn, whispered back, "We'll see."

After a couple of weeks had gone by, and Cindy had not had any indication that her father had worn the cologne, she asked her mother about it.

"I don't know, Cindy," Janet replied. "I haven't seen it since the day you gave it to him. Maybe it has disappeared to the same mysterious place where all the others have gone."

"But do you know if he has worn it?" Cindy asked.

"I haven't smelled it, if that's what you're asking," Janet replied.

At dinner that evening, Cindy asked her father if he enjoyed the cologne.

Her father nodded. "Absolutely. It's probably my favorite kind."

After dinner, as Cindy helped her mother wash the dishes, they talked about it.

"Mom, how could Dad say he loves the cologne, and yet we never smell it? Do you think that he took it to his office and only uses it at work? Is he trying to impress someone there?"

Janet smiled. "Cindy, what your father does with cologne may be a mystery, but the kind of man he is isn't. Your father is as simple a man as there is. He works hard and often says that the best men smell of sweat and dirt from hard work. I'm sure he doesn't wear it at his job any more than he wears it here. Perhaps it's just the thought of his daughter's love for him that makes it special to him."

That was not good enough for Cindy. It just ate at her not knowing what her father did with the cologne. So, she raised the issue with him again at dinner the next evening.

"So, Dad, why is the cologne I gave you one of your favorites?"

Her father smiled. "Honey, that stuff takes rust off of bolts like nothing I know of. It would be absolutely perfect if it didn't stink so bad, but I guess anything good has to have some defect."

And thus, the cologne mystery was solved.

Something New, Something Sweet

When we walked into the buffet restaurant, the first thing that caught Jason's eye was the chocolate fountain. It had three huge tiers with gallons of chocolate flowing over them.

"That's just about the most amazing thing ever!" he said.

This buffet lunch was the last part of our scouting high adventure. As we had planned the week, the boys made one request that was out of the norm from other high adventures I had been on. They had asked to eat out at some restaurants. The boys and leaders had worked hard on fundraising, putting flags at every home in our community on all of the main holidays. People who could afford to donate had been generous. So, amidst all the boating, fishing, and camping, we ate at a Mongolian grill and another restaurant famous for its big pancakes; we ended the week at the all-you-can-eat buffet.

While I was paying for our entrance into the buffet, Jason was busy checking out the chocolate fountain. By the time I joined everyone at our table, he had a plate full of chocolate-covered marshmallows and strawberries. He set it in front of me.

"What's this?" I asked.

"I did these for you," he replied.

"Why didn't you do them for yourself?"

"You know my parents don't want me to eat sugar," he said.

It was true that he avoided sugar, except for chocolate milk. Even so, he still had more energy than any boy I knew. I wondered what he would be like if he did eat sugar.

"They do look good," I said. "But I better eat other food first, or my blood sugar will spike."

I got a plate of salad and some roast and potatoes. When I finished that, I ate the chocolate-covered marshmallows and strawberries. I went back for shrimp and chicken and returned to find another plate of chocolate-covered strawberries. I didn't even have to ask who had done it.

"Jason, what's this?" I asked.

"It's so much fun dipping them in the chocolate; I made you some more."

I looked at my plate of food and the chocolate-covered strawberries, and I considered that I would need a bloat needle if I ate all of it.

"No more," I said. "I might be able to eat these, but don't you dare make me any more chocolate-covered anything."

I ate my shrimp and chicken and slowly made my way through the chocolate-covered strawberries. I had just finished the last one when Jason came back with an ice-cream cone with ice-cream about a foot high. He was carefully balancing it to keep it from falling. He held it out to me.

"What's this?" I asked.

"We're having a contest to see who can make the highest cone. So far, I'm winning."

I took it, but said, "No more, Jason. I mean it. I'm going to be sick now."

I hate to see food go to waste, so I slowly ate it. I had just reached the bottom and knew I couldn't even look at another food item when I saw Jason filling another ice cream cone. I went over to him.

"Who's that for?" I asked.

"You," he replied. "Someone beat my record, so I have to go higher."

"I am not eating it!" I said. "You make it; you eat it!"

"But I don't eat sugar," he replied.

"You have chocolate milk, and ice cream is just frozen chocolate milk, so it's yours," I replied.

He grinned and nodded. He piled that one higher than the one he made for me, and he ate it. He then made another one even higher and ate it, too.

When we headed home, I realized I had made a big mistake telling him to eat the ice cream. We had to ride home with him, and his energy turned nuclear. By the time we got home, I was not only sick, but I was also going crazy. It's no wonder his parents didn't want him eating sugar.

Hatchet Woman

I grew up on a ranch in the middle of nowhere in Idaho. Our nearest neighbors were a mile away in one direction, with no one living beyond us the opposite way. I could ride my horse out through the rangeland for miles and never see anyone. So, when I arrived in New York and was assigned to work in Buffalo, it was a whole new world for me.

"How do we get around?" I asked Walt, the young man with whom I was assigned to work.

"How did you get around at home?" he asked.

"A horse or pickup truck, mostly. Sometimes a tractor, if it entails farm work."

"Well, here you walk or take a bus," he replied.

My first bus trip across town was a new experience, and I almost lost Walt when we had to do a transfer. If I had, I probably would have never found my way back to the apartment and would have learned to sleep on the streets among the people our religious work often took us to. But Walt found me, and I was okay.

Our work took us into some tough neighborhoods as we tried to serve and help people. That's why when Walt first mentioned our landlady, it made me nervous. I saw her in her yard whacking at a bush with a big machete.

"Who's that?" I asked.

"Oh, that's Hatchet Woman," Walt replied. "She's our landlady."

The name Hatchet Woman made all sorts of ideas run through my mind. I decided it would be best to keep an eye on her. But Walt didn't seem to give her a second thought. And though over time I found her to be somewhat of a salty woman, the more I got to know her, the more I found her to be just an eccentric old lady. So, one day I asked Walt about the name.

"Oh, Hatchet Woman?" he replied. "It's a long story."

Walt told me he and the young man before me had come into the area looking for a place to stay. They found the ad for the small apartment and went to check it out. Betty, Hatchet Woman's real name, was very businesslike, and they soon agreed on a lease.

Walt said he quickly learned that when Betty was upset, she liked to take a shovel, a hoe, a machete, or a hatchet out to whack at weeds or overgrown shrubs in her yard. She said it made her feel better. But he said the way she went after the bushes was a bit unnerving.

Walt said one day he and the young man he was working with came home, and Betty was especially annoyed at something. She had a hatchet and was using it to hack away at a small tree that had started growing in the middle of her roses. As she chopped at the tree, she was getting cut up from the thorns.

"We considered helping her," Walt said, "but the way she was wielding that hatchet made us reconsider how safe that would be."

The two young men went to their apartment and watched Betty out the window.

"We didn't think she could see us through the window," Walt said. "But she would chop away for a while, and then she would look in our direction and let out a load of profanity. We were beginning to feel quite nervous, when after one of her outbursts, she stood up and threw the hatchet in our direction.

"The young man I worked with turned to me and said, 'I don't know about you, but I am out of here.' He headed down the stairs, out the door, and ran straight into Betty. She looked at us and said, 'Could you boys get my ladder and get my hatchet down for me?'"

Walt said they both froze and looked at her.

"Finally," Walt said, "I squeaked out 'Hatchet?' She nodded and said, 'I threw it at a squirrel, and the hatchet got stuck in the side of the house. Dang squirrels! Always chewing holes into the attic.'"

Walt grinned. "And that's how she got the name Hatchet Woman, but I would advise not calling her that to her face."

A Wonderful Day

My mother is 92 and has been without my father for about twelve years. Most of her friends have passed away, and even though she lives with my sister for part of the year, or is with other family, she still feels lonely without my father, her friends, and her parents and siblings who are gone.

With the Labor Day holiday coming up, she said she would love to do something different from the normal routine of her life. That was when I got the idea of having us all take her and drive the hour and a half to where she was born and raised. One of my daughters suggested that we have lunch at a buffet restaurant, too. It all sounded like a great day. The only problem was, I had so much to do, and I wondered if I could make it all work.

On Labor Day, I was up at 5:30 in the morning helping the scouts put flags up in front of every home in our rural community. When I got home, I did my homework for my doctoral classes, and before I finished, my mother was more than ready to go. We were soon on our way, and as we drove along, my mother told us stories.

"Over in that house was a friend of mine. Her name was Linda. Actually, it wasn't exactly that house. That is a new one. But that's where it was."

I handed my wife my phone and whispered for her to turn on the recorder. For an hour and a half, we drove there and recorded stories, interjected with her exclamation of how much something had changed since she had last been there. We went to the cemetery, and even though it was big, we quickly found where her family members were buried.

While my daughters and I cleaned around the tombstones, my mother continued to tell stories of each person, and my wife kept the recorder going. Once the grass was cleared from the graves, we drove by the university where my mother had gone to school. With how much it had changed, we were surprised how many buildings she knew, and she told stories about each one and the events that happened there.

We stopped at the buffet, and everyone overate—at least, I know I did. My mother said she enjoyed the meal more than any she had in a while and wouldn't need to eat for a week.

Our next stop was the home where she was born. I had never been there before, and the house was not there. In its place was a new home, but she told lots of stories of living there until she was seven. Then the depression came, and her father lost his job. The home was mostly paid off, and only had $400 left owed on it, but without an income, her parents lost it.

Our last stop was the farm her family moved to after they lost the first home. The house they built still stands. She told stories about growing up there as we drove slowly by. She didn't want to hurry, and indeed, even though I had a lot to do, I was willing to take even more time. But Mom was getting tired and needed some rest, so we finally headed home.

On the way home, Mom said very little. Some of the family were asleep, but she wasn't, and looking in the mirror, I could see she was deep in reminiscent thought. She had worked hard all her life, helped many people, and had ten children and raised nine of them. Life had sometimes been hard, but there was lots of love and good times, too.

When we got home, she held onto my arm as I carried her oxygen. Exhausted, she slumped into her favorite chair. It's then she shared her deepest thoughts of the day.

"Daris," she said, "it has been a wonderful day. I know I will soon go to be with my parents and your father. But I can't keep wondering what they will think of the life this old girl has lived."

I assured her they would be pleased, and as I left her to rest, I considered that it had been a wonderful day and time well spent.

Powder Puff Football

My daughter told me she was playing Powder Puff football. I found out the girls played against each other—it was much different from when I was in high school.

I remember Coach gathering us football players in the dressing room before practice on Thursday, the day before a big game. I thought he was going to give us a pep talk, but the topic was about the next week.

"Okay," he said, "Monday is the first day of Homecoming week, so first thing in the afternoon, before practice, we have the Powder Puff football game. Those of you who are starters will be playing, so come here right after you eat lunch. The rest of you are cheerleaders."

"Hey, Len," I said as we headed to practice, "what's Powder Puff football?"

"What rock did you crawl out from under?" Lenny replied. "Haven't you seen a Powder Puff game before?"

I shook my head. "I only started football in my junior year, and besides, my dad needed me for harvest every minute possible in the fall."

"Well, the starting football team plays against the girls," Lenny said.

"Won't the girls get hurt?" I asked.

"Don't worry," he replied. "Things are equalized in their favor, and they always win. In fact, the boys have never scored a point no matter how hard they've tried. You'll see."

On Monday afternoon, we went to the football field. We had a slight introduction before the game. The first thing I learned was that every boy had one arm, his dominant arm, tied behind his back. We all had flags in our back pockets. The girls were allowed to tackle or grab the flag. The boys could not tackle; they could only grab flags. It didn't take me long to see the challenge.

When the game started, the girls opted to receive. I got ready to kick off. But just before I could, our teammates on the sideline, who were all dressed in cheerleading costumes from their mothers, swarmed us, and the kick went nowhere. The girls had the ball at midfield. The girls had no rules, and after the ball was hiked, all girls except the ball carrier grabbed a guy and held onto his jersey so he couldn't do anything. Two held onto me. That was when I realized there were more than the normal eleven girls on the field.

With the other girls holding onto us, the girl with the ball made a touchdown. It was then our turn to receive. But have you ever tried to catch a ball or pick one up with one hand tied behind your back? It was a comedy of errors, and the crowd roared with laughter. We had barely gotten the ball when the girls all grabbed the boy who had it and piled on him. We tried to defend, but it's hard with one hand tied behind your back and girls grabbing your jersey.

The game went the same way all afternoon, and the score was 41 to zero. We had possession and came to a huddle for the last play of the game.

"Okay," Lenny said. "We can't win, but we can still make history if we score a point."

We decided to do a big fake. The quarterback would act like he was giving the ball to the halfback, then all of the team, except the quarterback and me, would move to the right with the halfback. The quarterback and I would go left and move quickly down the field.

The fake worked beautifully. All fifteen or so girls moved with the team, leaving an open field in front of the quarterback and me. With me flanking him, getting in the way of any girl who came at us, the quarterback moved quickly toward the goal line. It seemed sure that we would score the first points ever for guys playing Powder Puff football.

But we forgot about all the boys in the cheerleader outfits on the edge of the field. Just about the time we reached the ten-yard line, the boys flooded onto the field and took both the quarterback and me down. Then the girls all piled on to end the game.

And so, the score stayed 41 to 0. We didn't go down in history, we just went down, and we still laugh about it.

Perfect Sisters

They were the perfect sisters. They were both kind and pretty, and both were cheerleaders. Sally was my age, and Martha was a year younger. I had never seen them angry at each other, and a person would be wise not to cross one of them, or he might be facing the wrath of both. I had never seen two more devoted siblings.

"Sally," I said one day, "how do you and Martha get along so well? My brother and I are definitely not as good of friends as the two of you are."

Sally smiled. "I don't really know. We almost never argue. Martha is my best friend."

I watched them through two years of school and knew that it was not just an act. They were genuinely best friends. It was no surprise that after Sally was hired at the local hamburger joint, Martha soon was working there, too, and they worked amazingly well together.

One night, I was asked to pick up a couple of gallons of root beer for a party. The hamburger place where Sally and Martha worked sold it fresh from the tap. So, an hour or so before the party was to start, I made my way over there. I hoped for a chance to have a casual visit with the girls while I was getting my order filled.

I was surprised to see the two of them working alone. It was dinner time, and usually there were at least six employees. But for some reason, Sally and Martha were working alone and running as fast as they could. Sally was cooking orders, and in between, she would run out and serve. Martha was taking orders and serving. Both girls were tired and sweaty.

There was a huge line of people waiting for food. I sat on a stool at the counter.

"Be with you in a minute," Sally said.

"No hurry," I said. "There are a lot of people ahead of me."

The girls worked hard, but for a long time, the line didn't go down at all. But eventually, the dinner rush slowed, and they started to catch up. A couple of other workers came, which also helped. But one customer, who had been waiting a little while, let both girls have his ire as they gave him his order.

I felt it was unfair because they were doing their best. But the man was soon gone, and Martha turned to the last lady in line. The lady ordered an ice-cream cone.

"Sally, can you get that?" Martha asked in a tense voice. "I have a couple of other orders to serve."

"Get it yourself," Sally replied. "I have to go back to the kitchen."

Sally went to the kitchen, and Martha let out an exasperated sigh. Martha filled the two orders she had ready and was just getting the cone made when Sally came out. Sally saw the lady still standing there waiting, and Sally turned to her sister.

"Martha, for heaven's sake, don't you have that cone ready yet?"

"Lay off!" Martha said, "Unless you want this cone in your face."

A couple more workers showed up, so Sally turned her attention to me. Quite angrily, she asked, "So, what can I get you?"

"Two gallons of root beer," I replied. And as Sally turned to get them, I added, "And can I get that service with a smile?"

She turned to me and scowled, "Don't push your luck."

Sally brought me the root beer, then asked, "Is there anything else?"

"Yes," I replied. "It's the first time I have seen two certain sisters angry with each other."

Sally and Martha looked at each other sheepishly as I continued. "But I was just thinking, if the two of you can take a break, I'd love to buy us some ice-cream cones so we can visit."

The other workers said they could handle things, so I purchased the ice-cream, and the three of us sat down to visit.

As the girls took a much-needed break, Sally said, "I hope you don't think we always act like that."

"I know you don't," I said, "and you had a good reason, anyway. But I still didn't get my service with a smile."

They both smiled, and then Sally laughed and said, "You still might be pushing your luck."

Indoor Plumbing

Goren and Lilly had been married for just over a year, and Lilly was growing annoyed with Goren. He had promised that he would put indoor plumbing into the house after they were married, but he hadn't. Lilly was tired of bathing at the hand pump in the summer and dragging water into the house to bathe in the winter. Goren didn't seem to mind, but then, he didn't wash as much as he should, anyway. Working with cattle was dirty work, and he always came home smelling like cows.

"Goren," Lilly said one night, "things have got to change. We've been married a year, and you still haven't put in the indoor plumbing."

"I haven't had time," Goren replied.

"It needs to be a priority," Lilly said. "And you need to make sure you bathe every time you come home at night. It's really hard to keep the house smelling nice for when people come to visit."

"But no one comes to visit," Goren replied.

That was true. They lived on a cattle ranch, and the nearest neighbor lived about ten miles away.

"Well, they might," Lilly said. "And we still live here and should have it nice. I want you to promise me that when you come home each night, you will strip off your clothes for me to wash, and then go bathe at the pump before you come into the house."

Goren reluctantly promised, and he also said he would get the plumbing done. But another six months passed, and nothing changed. He kept coming into the house smelling like he'd been dragged through a barnyard.

Then one fall evening, Goren drove into the yard. Lilly had just done the wash and was airing out the house. Goren had been branding cattle and smelled worse than ever. The smell wafted through the windows. By the time he reached the door, Lilly was there to meet him.

"You are not setting foot in my nice clean house until you have had a bath," she said. "Strip off your clothes and go to the pump."

Goren sighed but did as instructed. He went to the pump while Lilly picked up the clothes using a couple of sticks. She hauled them around behind the house and dumped them into the barrel of wash water. She had just entered the house when she saw a dust cloud about a mile away. It was a telltale sign that someone was coming down the old dirt road.

Goren had seen it too, and he streaked toward the house to get some clothes. Lilly saw him coming, and she was not about to have him come in and stink up the house when visitors were coming. She beat him to the door and locked it. Goren pounded on the door, but Lilly was not inclined to unlock it until he finished his bath. Goren must have realized it, and with the pickup approaching quickly, he dashed around to the back of the house. But Lilly had already locked that door.

Goren was desperate as the pickup pulled to a stop in the yard. He decided to hide in the outhouse. He peeked out and saw two ministers from the church step from the pickup. Lilly unlocked the front door and invited the men in. As they entered the house, they said they had come to visit with Goren.

"Um, he's indisposed right now," Lilly said.

"We'll be on our way, then," one of the men replied. "But it's a long way back. May I use your outhouse first?"

Lilly didn't know Goren was in there and said yes. Goren panicked. But hearing the men's voices from inside the house, Goren realized the windows were still open. He slipped out of the outhouse and dashed for the opposite side of the house as Lilly and the two men came back outside. Goren climbed on an old milk can and had just stuck one foot through the window when the window crashed down on him, causing him to slip and trapping his foot. The falling window had

19

broken out some glass, and the noise brought Lilly running back in, with the two men close behind. And there Goren hung, upside down, in his compromised state.

Within a week, Lilly had indoor plumbing, because Goren suddenly felt it was a priority.

A Desk Full of Memories

As we moved furniture recently, a small white desk brought a flood of memories to my mind. My wife, Donna, and I had only been married about a year and a half and had a two-month-old daughter. I was struggling to work my way through college and take care of my little family. What work I found was usually part-time, paid minimum wage, and was seldom steady.

Donna tried to save money in every way she could. She purchased an old sewing machine at a garage sale and sewed our clothes. Much of the work I found was hard, physical work, and I often tore holes in my clothes, especially my pants. Donna patched them until even my patches had patches on them.

But it was hard for me knowing Donna had no desk at which to sew. The only surface we had in our apartment was the small kitchen table. It was hard to lay everything on it, only to have to move it when we ate, and it didn't fit much more than the sewing machine. I would come home from a long day of work, and Donna would be sitting on the floor sewing, with the baby close by. It was cute, but it was hard on Donna's back and made her tired. I decided to try to get her a sewing desk. Everywhere I went, I looked for an inexpensive desk at secondhand stores and at every garage sale but found nothing we could afford.

Then, one night, we went to a charity auction. I scraped together every penny we had and counted twenty dollars. I was hoping to buy some tools to fix our small pickup. It was our only transportation, and it was not running well. At the auction, we added the Jell-O salad that Donna made with the other potluck food and then paid the five-dollar donation for the meal. After we ate, we wandered among the donated items before the auction started.

I found an old set of tools that I thought would work for what I needed. They had a suggested starting bid of five dollars, but then something else caught my attention. I saw Donna standing by a nice little desk. It wasn't just any desk; it was a sewing desk with drawers made for bobbins and other useful items. I saw her look at the suggested bid and disappointedly turn away. I went over and looked at the tag. It suggested a thirty-dollar opening bid. My heart sank. The desk would be perfect, but we only had fifteen dollars left.

The auctioneer started and moved through the items quickly. When he got to the tools and started the bid at ten dollars, I almost bid. But somehow, I couldn't do it. All I could think of was the desk. The tools sold for twelve dollars, and Donna asked why I didn't bid.

"I'm not sure they were what I needed," I replied.

That was true, but there was a more important reason. When the desk came up for bid, the auctioneer asked, "Who will bid forty dollars?" No one said anything, so he dropped it to thirty-five, then thirty, then twenty-five. Still no one bid, so he moved to something else.

When he had sold almost everything else and paused for a moment, I slipped up to him.

"Are you going to sell the desk?" I asked.

"No one seemed to want to start the bidding," he replied.

"I would have, but I don't have as much as you wanted," I said. "But I would like it for my wife."

"How much do you want to bid?" he asked.

"Fifteen dollars is all I have," I replied, "and I will bid it all."

He looked at me and seemed to realize that I was a struggling college student, and he smiled. "You've got yourself a desk."

He motioned to the lady marking down the sold items, and she handed me the paper to pay for the desk. But after everything else was sold, a man asked about it. The auctioneer told the man the desk was sold.

"But no one even bid on it," the man complained. "I planned

to, but I didn't want to start."

The auctioneer turned and smiled at me, and then said to the man, "I doubt you could have beat the bid, because you'd have to give everything you had."

As we recently moved the old desk, I think Donna remembered, too, because she looked at it, smiled, and hugged me.

A Pregnancy Adventure

✦

One of my daughters is expecting a baby, and as with each new addition to our family, we are really excited. There are only a few weeks left, so I wasn't surprised when my cell phone started beeping every few seconds. I looked to see that everyone was guessing the day and time of the arrival, along with the baby's weight and length. It is a tradition in our family that each person who is closest in one of the four categories wins a candy bar.

When my mother came over for Sunday dinner, I asked her if she wanted to make a guess.

"I don't think so," she said. "I can just buy myself a candy bar if I want one."

"But it's the sense of adventure," I told her.

She grunted and said, "You're a man. What do you know about adventure when it comes to having a baby?"

"Well," I said, "we have had a few adventures getting to the hospital and a few more once we got there."

"Hmpf," my mother said. "Let me tell you about adventure."

Those at the dinner turned their attention to her as she told her story.

"After I had had my fifth child, I knew pretty well how my pregnancies would go. They had all been the same. I would be in miserable labor for two days, and then I would feel a change in the intensity. When that happened, I knew it wasn't going to be long, and I needed to get to the hospital. So, when my sixth child was born, and I had been in labor for two days, I was careful to pay attention to that change. When it came, I had your father rush me to the hospital.

"In those days, men were not allowed into the mother's hospital room or in the delivery room until the baby was born. Your father had to stay out in the waiting area. Once I was settled into my bed, the nurse checked me. 'You're not anywhere near ready,' she said. 'You might as well go back

24

home for a while.'

"I told her I knew my pregnancies better than she did, and it wouldn't be long. She was a young nurse who was just new out of school, and she felt she knew better than me. She just grunted, rolled her eyes, and left the room. The contractions were intense, and about fifteen minutes later, I knew the baby was coming. I pressed the nurse's button, but no one came. I continued to press it, but still, no one came for about fifteen minutes. Finally, the young nurse returned.

"I asked, 'Didn't you hear the buzzer?' She said she had, but she hadn't worried about it because she knew I was nowhere near ready. She took her time checking me, and when she did, she yelled, 'The baby is almost here!' She then ran to the door and yelled down the hall for help.

"Meanwhile, the young nurse decided she should give me some gas to help with the pain. I told her there wasn't time for that, but she insisted. She got the mask and turned on the gas. In her state of anxiety, she felt everything was going too slow. She said, 'This dang gas must not be working because I can't smell anything.' She turned it up as high as it would go but still thought it wasn't working, so she turned the mask toward herself and promptly passed out onto the floor.

"A short time later, another nurse came in, saw the young nurse on the floor and the baby coming, and she hit the code-red button. Soon, people were scurrying around, knocking into each other with the gas still filling the room, until everyone started feeling loopy. I thought we were all going to pass out. Finally, someone thought to shut the gas off, everyone settled down, and the baby came."

Mom finished with, "Now, that was a baby delivery adventure. I bet you can't match that."

"Well," I said, "once when one of our babies was coming, Donna dug her nails into my hand so hard I almost bled."

Mom just said, "Hmpf. Wimp."

An Old Friend

Recently, I was traveling a long, dusty road when I stopped at a place in the middle of nowhere. The road from our high school in St. Anthony to the one in Salmon where we often competed ran through a long, barren stretch of road. The trip on a school bus was about three hours and seemed to go forever. There was lots of sagebrush with a few mountains to add interest.

About halfway between the two schools was a small town. It was small even by Idaho standards. In fact, it was so small that it consisted of only one house and a café. But as small as it was, it was on the map. Blue Dome, it was called.

Probably the reason it was on the map was because there wasn't anything else for miles around. It was a lone outpost in an area with interesting trails leading up into mountains with intriguing names like Diamond Peak, Copper Mountain, and Skull Canyon. But I found my greatest interest in the lives of the old couple who ran the café.

I was a young teenager when I first met them. I was traveling on my first athletic trip. We had a long day of wrestling, and then headed home at around 9:00 at night. It was late when we made it to Blue Dome, but the open sign still showed, so our bus pulled to a stop. As the team members spilled out of the bus and into the café, I looked at the hours that were posted and realized the café was just ready to close. But after we entered, the little old couple worked hard cooking and serving as if they planned to stay open all night.

I didn't have much money, so I sat on a stool at the counter apart from the others and ordered a water.

"Nothing else?" the old man asked.

"I don't have a lot of money," I said.

After everyone else was served, he came back over and asked if there was anything else he could do for me.

"Well," I slowly said, "there is one thing. I'd love to know your story and the story of this place."

He smiled. "I sometimes get that request from adults, but I think you're the first young person who has ever asked."

My memory has faded over the years, but I think I remember that his name was John. He told me how he met his wife and how they settled in this out-of-the-way place. He talked about his family and about running the café. When my teammates needed something, John would slip away to serve or to help his wife and then return and continue his stories.

Once everyone else was heading to the bus, I put the little bit of money I had on the counter.

"Water's free," John said.

"Then take that as a tip for the stories," I said. "I would come here just for them."

John smiled and brought his wife over and introduced her to me. She looked as old as John, but to see their eyes sparkle when they looked at each other was more beautiful than any young love.

All the others were on the bus when Coach came in and called me to hurry. I joined the others, and they teased me about my "old friends." But on the way home, I thought about the wonderful couple I had met.

After that, every sports bus I traveled in on that long road stopped at Blue Dome, and I spent my time visiting with John. On the last one, as everyone hurried out, John stopped me before I left.

"Have you signed our wall?" he asked.

I looked at where he was pointing and saw a wall with hundreds of names. I shook my head.

He handed me a marker. "You better sign it."

The team impatiently waited while I signed the wall. And I received the usual teasing, but I didn't care. I liked my old friends. But it was only about a week later when I read the bad news in the paper. The café had burned down, and John had died in the fire.

And now, though it has been a long time, sometimes when I travel that road, I will stop at Blue Dome. There is nothing left to see but a crumbling old cabin and the café's foundation, but there are lots of memories, and I like to take the time to stop and remember an old friend.

No One Knows Why

✦

I played offensive guard and defensive tackle on my high school football team. On special teams, I was on both receiving and on kickoff. I was almost always on the field. Then one day, my line coach saw me kick the football. The kicker had been challenging and mocking everyone, saying they couldn't kick as well as he could, so my line coach had me take the challenge, but only after the head coach was watching. So, after I kicked the ball past the end zone into the parking lot, I became the new kickoff person.

I mostly loved to kick off, but there was one thing I hated about it. Our head coach, Coach Dale, said I had to stay back and be the last defender. From playing in my other position, I was used to going quickly down the field, usually getting in on the tackle. As the kicker, I had an even better chance of getting in on the tackle because I was at the front, I was going full steam, and I also knew where I was aiming the kick.

We were doing our first kickoff in the second game after I became the kicker, when I forgot Coach Dale's admonition. I kicked the ball into the end zone, and by the time the ball carrier came out, I was at the five-yard line to meet him. I didn't tackle him alone, but I was a big part of it. However, when the play ended, Coach Dale called me over, and he wasn't happy.

"Howard, how many times have I told you, the kicker is to stay back and be the last defense?"

"Sorry, Coach," I replied. "I always forget. I'm used to going after the tackle."

"What will happen if the ball carrier gets through, and you aren't there to stop him?"

"But why can't someone else be the final defender?" I asked. "After I kick, I already have full momentum heading down the field, and I've almost always been in on the tackle."

Coach stood there, seemingly stunned by what I said. I wondered if it was because I dared question him. I didn't mean to. I had only started football my junior year, and there were a lot of things I didn't know. But I always asked a lot of questions, so I thought he would have been used to it. But when he spoke, his voice betrayed no anger, but confusion.

"You know, Howard, I don't know why the kicker is always the one who stays back. It has just been the case on every team I've played on. Just keep playing, and we'll talk about it at halftime."

I went in to play my defensive position, getting into place shortly before the ball was snapped. Through that half, I kicked off a few more times, and each time, I had to carefully remember to hold back to be the last defender. I really hated it. By halftime, I was about to ask Coach if the previous kicker could go in to kick instead of me so I could go after the tackle. But true to his word, Coach Dale brought up the question of why the kicker was the last defender. As soon as we were settled into the locker room, he turned to the line coach.

"Coach Bahler, Howard asked why the kicker has to be the one who is the last defender and can't go for the tackle. Can you tell him?"

Coach Bahler had the same stunned look that Coach Dale had had. He shrugged.

"I don't know, other than that is the way it was done on every team I played on."

Coach Dale then turned to the third coach. "Coach Smith, how about you?"

Coach Smith shrugged, too. "Same thing for me."

The last coach was Coach Jackson. He had played some semi-pro football and was old and retired. He wasn't paid but volunteered his time.

"I'll tell you why the kicker has always been the last defender," Coach Jackson said. "It's because he's usually the only one who can do his job; he's usually small and thin, and no one wants him to get hurt." The coaches all looked at me, and then Coach Jackson said, "For you to hold Howard back because you don't want him to get hurt, and then to put him in on both the offensive and defensive lines, seems kind of stupid."

"What's stupid," Coach Dale said, "is that we've been doing something that has always been done without even knowing why."

With that, he turned to me and said, "Howard, you can

go for the tackle, and we'll have someone else be the last defender."

And for me that day, the kickoff suddenly got a whole lot better.

The New Job

✦

We youth leaders in our community had just finished going through the straw maze and were waiting for some of the youth to make multiple forays through when the conversation turned to the jobs the teenagers had been able to find. As we talked about this subject, Susan told us about a unique job her son, Jace, had had.

He had come bursting into the house one day, filled with excitement. "Mom, guess what? I have a job!"

Jace was young enough that Susan had her concerns. "And just what is this job?" she asked.

"You know how Mrs. Owen raises lots of parrots?" Jace asked. Susan nodded, so Jace continued. "She has asked if I would like to help her train them to speak. It will only pay minimum, but it would be almost every night, and it would be steady work. Besides, she doesn't live far away."

Mrs. Owen was their neighbor and lived around the corner. She loved birds. Her whole garage was full of birds, many she had raised from eggs. She had just about every kind of parrot or parrot-related bird a person could imagine or legally own. Susan could see why this job captured the imagination of her young son. But how does a person help teach a bird to speak?

"Just what would your job entail?" Susan asked.

Jace shrugged. "I don't know exactly. I have never taught a bird to speak before. But I'm sure it can't be that hard. I think that I will probably sit in the room with the birds and just say certain phrases over and over."

"But why does she need you to do that?" Susan asked. "It would seem she could do that herself."

Jace's eyebrows knit together, and he shrugged. "I'd never thought of that. Maybe she's just too busy."

"She's retired, Jace, and the birds are her life. I'm sure she's not too busy."

"Well," Jace said slowly, as if thinking out loud. "I've heard that birds learn to speak in the voice of the person they hear. Maybe she has some male birds, and she doesn't want them to speak like girls."

Susan smiled at the thought. She was quite sure it didn't matter if a bird spoke with a female voice or male voice, but she couldn't think of any other reason.

Susan trusted her neighbor implicitly, so she didn't see any reason Jace couldn't take the job. However, Susan's curiosity was such that she decided to join Jace when he went to his first night of work.

When they reached Mrs. Owen's house, the old widow led them into her garage. Susan was given a chair so she could sit and watch. Mrs. Owen was carrying a bag in one hand, and she had Jace stand beside her.

Mrs. Owen turned to Jace. "Jace, say hello."

Jace looked stunned and said nothing, so Mrs. Owen repeated the request. Jace said hello, and Mrs. Owen stuck a treat up to his lips, which he ate.

Mrs. Owen then turned to the bird. "Patty, say hello."

The bird eyed both Jace and Mrs. Owen suspiciously. Mrs. Owen made the request again, but still, the bird said nothing. Once more, Mrs. Owen turned to Jace.

"Jace, say hello."

Jace said hello, and Mrs. Owen gave him a treat. She then turned to the bird and once more said, "Patty, say hello."

Susan smiled, watching this for over an hour, and eventually, a few of the birds caught the hang of it, said hello, and received their own treat.

When Susan finished with the story, I said, "That has got to be one of the most interesting jobs I've ever heard of."

Susan nodded. "The only downside was that, for Jace, the job was quite fattening."

Going Solo

Jacob loved music. He sang while he milked the cows, changed sprinkler pipes, or rode his horse. But he lacked confidence in his ability. One of his brothers had heard him singing once and had made fun of him, so Jacob was careful to only sing when he thought no one else was around.

There wasn't much in the way of music in Jacob's small, rural community. The high school that he attended didn't have a band, a choir, or anything. But in his junior year, a new math teacher was hired who also had a minor in music. She was going to teach a choir class.

Jacob was thrilled at the thought of having a music class each day. But then he realized others might hear him sing, and that scared him. He thought about it for a long time. He would get the determination to join the class only to have his resolve waver. When it came time for registration, he learned that there was no audition. The teacher was willing to take anyone, especially boys. Grades were based solely on attendance in class and at the concerts.

Jacob decided he could just mouth the words, and no one would know. He could fake like he was singing and just enjoy listening to the others. So, with a little bit of trepidation, he signed up. However, as soon as the teacher started class the first day, Jacob realized he would at least have to sing something so the teacher could determine what group to put him in.

As each choir member sang a short phrase from "America the Beautiful," and the teacher listened, Jacob began to tremble. But he realized that most of the class didn't know much about music, either. Oh, there were a few who seemed to. And there were others who didn't sound that good but were full of confidence. When it was Jacob's turn, he sang so quietly that the teacher had to move up close to him and have him sing again.

"You sound like you're a baritone, Jacob," she said. "You could probably do either tenor or bass, so I will see where I need you most."

"What's a baritone?" Jacob asked one of his friends.

"It is a barely tone, which means a person can barely sing," the boy replied with a laugh.

"That beats being tenor—ten or eleven notes off," another boy joked.

Jacob tried to smile at their humor, but it wasn't making him feel better.

As the weeks wore on, Jacob loved the music. He started out mouthing the words, but sometimes he became so caught up in the joy of what they were doing that he forgot and actually sang.

One day, Jacob was late to school, as usual, after milking the cows, and he missed the beginning announcements. The teacher passed the roll sheet around in class, and when the paper came, Jacob signed it. But a few minutes later, another paper came.

"What's this?" he asked the boy standing next to him.

"The roll, duh," the boy answered.

"Then what was the last paper?" Jacob asked.

"It was to sign up for a solo," the boy replied. "If you ever came on time, you'd know."

Jacob was so frightened he couldn't even think of the words to mouth them all class period. When class was over, he hurried to the teacher and explained his mistake and that he couldn't sing a solo.

"Jacob," she said, "I know that a lot of times you just mouth the words, but I can tell when you sing, and you actually have a beautiful voice. I hope you will reconsider."

The teacher promised to work with Jacob during lunch hour. Added to that, Melonie, a girl Jacob liked, would sing the female solo part. The three of them met each day, and Jacob sang with more and more confidence. Their duet at the concert turned out well, and they received a standing ovation.

Through the years, Jacob and Melonie continued to sing together, and after high school graduation, they were married. As he took Melonie into his arms on their wedding day, he told her that signing that solo paper by accident was the best mistake he ever made. She smiled and said she was glad he had.

The Weight Loss Center

Sam was tired of working his boring job. He wanted to strike out and become an entrepreneur. He had a great idea for a business venture. He was going to start a fitness and weight loss center. He loved to work with people on losing weight, and he had trained as a fitness coach. It was the perfect business for him. But the first thing he had to find was a place that was big enough for a gym.

Sam searched all over and found a basement in a business building. It had a high ceiling that was high enough to put some basketball hoops at one end. He could put exercise equipment in the other. It would need quite a bit of work, but the rent was cheap. He also felt that the businesses that were in the upper two floors of the building would draw people in.

Sam continued working his job, but the minute he got off work each day, he was working on his newly rented hall. He was cleaning, painting, and making it look inviting. He used his savings to buy some exercise bikes, treadmills, and weight machines. He hoped to add more later, but he felt it would give him a good start. He took out a small loan to pay the wages of the employees and other expenses for the first six months.

It seemed like forever to Sam before his business was ready, but finally, the grand-opening day arrived. He had a newspaper reporter come, and the mayor even did a ribbon-cutting. Sam offered the first month free or six months at half-price. His business boomed, and he was doing well, but there was something that really troubled him. His customers didn't seem to be losing any weight at all. In fact, some of them seemed to be gaining weight.

Sam consulted all his books from his training. Everything he was doing seemed to be right. None of his customers complained too much about the lack of weight loss, but he was sure that his business couldn't sustain itself with the numbers he was seeing. He tried everything he could think of and decided he needed to seek some outside help.

Sam went to one of his professors who had trained him as a fitness coach. Sam explained his dilemma and asked his professor if he would mind coming and spending an hour or so watching Sam work with his customers. The professor kindly agreed, and the next evening, he came at the appointed hour.

The professor seemed pleased with the work Sam had put into his business. He looked around and commented that he felt the equipment was sufficient for the job. But as Sam started training customers, the professor seemed occupied with other things. He kept walking around the gym as if searching for something. He must have found what he was looking for because he then walked to the exit and watched people who were leaving.

Sam was somewhat annoyed, wondering why the professor wasn't watching the workouts Sam was having people do, but Sam didn't dare question his professor. After about a half-hour of watching people leave, the professor returned to Sam.

"I'm pretty sure I know what your problem is, Sam," the professor said.

"What?" Sam asked.

The professor led Sam to a vent near the ceiling. "Sam, what is above that vent?"

Sam thought about it, considering the layout of the businesses on the nest floor. "That would be Antonio's Pizza Parlor," Sam replied.

"Just as I thought," the professor said. "This place smells of cheese and garlic. How can anyone concentrate on working out in a place that smells like the pizza center of Italy? And you know what else I noticed? The minute your customers leave, they head right upstairs and put back on every ounce they burned off."

Sam couldn't believe he hadn't thought of that. He got the vent rerouted outside, and immediately his customers' weight loss started to increase. To thank his professor, Sam invited him out for dinner. Of course, they ate at Antonio's. As Sam finished his last piece of wonderful pizza, he understood even better why his customers hadn't been losing weight.

An Unusual Assignment

It was the day after Thanksgiving. As a police officer, Samuel was preparing to go on patrol, but he had to fill out the required reports first. Paperwork was the thing he hated most. He much preferred to be out on the streets. He finished his reports and looked at his assignment. He was going to be working in a poor section of the city.

If there was one place Samuel liked to work, it was that section of town. He had made lots of friends in that area. Even though there was more crime there because of the poverty, the people whom he had come to know were more inclined to stop and visit, and it made work go by faster. When he worked in the rich areas of town, too often, people were so caught up in their fast-paced lives that he never got more than a nod from them before they hurried on their way.

Samuel was just putting on his coat when he heard someone call his name. Samuel turned around, and there stood his sergeant. Samuel's heart sank, thinking he was going to be assigned some more paperwork.

"Officer Nakamura," the sergeant said, "could you use a sandwich before you head out?"

This statement took Samuel by surprise. Usually, his sergeant was all business. Samuel stood there for a minute, unable to speak. When he finally did speak, he just said, "A sandwich, Sir?"

The sergeant nodded. "Yes. Turkey or ham, to be exact."

Samuel hardly knew what to say, so he just sputtered, "Uh, yeah, I suppose a sandwich would be nice."

As the sergeant handed Samuel a sandwich, he sighed. "My wife expected a lot of family members to come yesterday, but the storm forced most of them to turn back. She had cooked two turkeys and a ham and made enough rolls to feed an army. She said she's not about to eat leftovers for a month, so she made them all into sandwiches and told me to give them away."

Samuel took the sandwich and took a bite. "This is very good, Sir. Thank you."

"Yeah, she's a good cook," the sergeant replied. "But I was just ready to get off work when I remembered the sandwiches. I don't dare go home until I have given them all away."

The sergeant started back to his desk, and Samuel started to button up his coat. Suddenly, the sergeant stopped and turned back around.

"What am I doing?" the sergeant said. "I don't have to give the sandwiches away. I can just assign you to do it."

"How many sandwiches are there?" Samuel asked.

"Three huge coolers full," the sergeant replied, pointing to the coolers by his desk. "You can just put the empty coolers back by my desk when you're done."

"But I was going out on a walking route," Samuel replied.

"Not anymore," the sergeant replied. "You'll need to take the patrol car."

With a nod, the sergeant said, "Happy after-Thanksgiving Day," and he quickly left.

Samuel looked in the first cooler and figured there were well over a hundred sandwiches in it. The other coolers were stuffed full as well. He wondered how and to whom he could give that many sandwiches. But then he smiled as he realized how stupid that thought was.

He loaded the coolers into the patrol car and headed to his assigned area. He stopped first by an old basketball court where teenagers were playing ball.

"Hey, anybody like a sandwich?" Samuel called out.

Soon, he had given out a few dozen sandwiches to some appreciative young people. Samuel stopped next at a place where homeless people hung out and were warming themselves around a fire. Though some people quickly disappeared at the site of his patrol car, they just as quickly came back when they heard he was offering free sandwiches.

Samuel continued passing out sandwiches wherever he went, to the old, to children in threadbare coats, and to everyone he met. His shift ended before the sandwiches were gone, but he continued until every last one was given away.

When Samuel came to work the next day, his sergeant apologized for giving him such a strange assignment. But Samuel just smiled and told what he had done.

"If your wife ever cooks too much, I'd be happy to give it away again."

After the sergeant told his wife about it, she made it an annual tradition to cook too much and make the leftovers into sandwiches. And Samuel looked forward to sharing the food on his beat. It was one of the few reports he looked forward to writing about.

It's a Beautiful Day

✦

My old friend, Bill, walked into church, and I smiled. It was good to see him. Bill is in his eighties and is one of the most positive people I know.

I went over and shook his hand. "Today is a great day, huh, Bill?"

He shook my hand heartily. "Yes, today is a beautiful day."

I'm sure those standing around us wondered about our unusual conversation, especially since it was freezing cold with a biting wind. But the reason for our strange conversation went back to a previous one that I had had with Bill a few years earlier.

I was having some challenges in my life. I had been given some new assignments at work that were taking a lot of time. I was also the editor of the university research magazine, and some people were quite vocal about their displeasure with me and the articles I chose to include in the publication. As a family, we also had some financial setbacks that were weighing on my mind.

On that particular day, I walked into church and ran into Bill. He shook my hand vigorously and said, "Isn't it a beautiful day?"

"You think so?" I said, feeling somewhat doubtful.

The day was overcast, a sleety rain was falling, and it was miserably cold.

"Yes," Bill replied, "it's a wonderful day. And do you know how I can tell if it's a wonderful day?"

"How?" I asked, his enthusiasm beginning to rub off on me.

"I get up each morning," Bill said, "and I read the newspaper immediately. The first thing I read is the obituaries. And do you know why I read the obituaries first?"

"Why?" I asked.

"Because if my name isn't there, I know it's going to be a great day."

Bill laughed and laughed at that. I laughed, too, and my problems seemed to disperse. But around a month ago, I found out Bill had an accident. He had been using his tractor to split firewood. It was a cold day, so he was in his shop with the door closed. He began to realize that the air was getting choked with exhaust, and he needed some fresh air. He walked to the switch to open the garage door, but just before he reached it, he passed out face down in the dirt.

Luckily, when Bill didn't come into the house for dinner as expected, his sweet wife went looking for him. She got her son to help, and when they found him, they quickly opened the door and called 911. Miraculously, the first volunteer emergency responders had oxygen. When I learned what had happened, I went to visit Bill. He was home from the hospital but still struggling to breathe, even with oxygen.

He was asleep when I came. I hated to wake him, but his wife said Bill would be disappointed if he missed getting to visit with me, so she gently patted him.

Bill slowly opened his eyes, and when he saw me, he smiled.

"It's still a great day, Bill," I said. "But just barely. It came close to not being a good one for you."

He smiled weakly. "A little too close."

He wasn't out of the woods yet at that point. But over time, he gradually started to get better. That was the reason I was so happy to see him when he walked into church.

Some of his positive attitude has taken hold of me, especially as his comment has lingered with me and has given me a different perspective about life. Each day when I get up, I say to myself, "It's a beautiful day," and I don't even have to read the obituaries to know it.

Detention Math

The math teacher was trying to teach about solving story problems using variables, but no one was listening to her because Dean was too busy making fun of the problem.

". . . and does anyone ever ask why Janet had forty watermelons? No, they just . . ."

"Dean," the teacher said sternly, "I'm trying to teach a lesson here. And do you know why I can't?"

"Because you don't know the material?" Dean replied with a smirk.

Dean soon found himself sitting in detention waiting for the principal. When the principal came out of his office, he looked at Dean and sighed.

"Here it is, the first week of school, and isn't this already the second time this week, Dean?"

"Third," Dean replied. "But who's counting? I'm sure not. I can't seem to get anywhere with numbers."

"Mrs. Sanderson says that is because you tell too many stories," the principal said.

"Well, maybe if I understood what the X she was talking about, she would know Y," Dean replied.

Dean laughed at his joke, but a person has to see the variables X and Y written to know for sure why it was funny. Yet, the principal seemed to catch it and even laughed.

"Dean," the principal said, "you're a smart boy. There's no reason you should be having this much trouble in math."

"I guess it's just that the teacher and I are not connecting," Dean said.

They talked for a while longer, and then the bell rang.

"Head to your next class," the principal said. "And try to not make my office your permanent residence."

The next day when Dean walked into math class, he was late. He had to do chores and missed the bus. The teacher was not allowed to mark a student late if they rode the bus, and the bus was late, so she asked, "Dean, did you ride the bus?"

"Nope," Dean said. "I rode a camel."

When the principal walked out of his office and saw Dean sitting there, he sighed. "Class only just started, Dean. How could you be here already?"

"The teacher asked me to find her X, so I told her if her X left her, she should find out Y and try to move on with her life, because her X probably wasn't coming back."

As Dean grinned, the principal shook his head, but Dean saw the hint of a smile. The principal went around behind his desk, sat down, and turned to face Dean.

"So, how do we get you to learn math, Dean?"

Dean shook his head. "Putting letters into equations makes no sense to me."

"How about I try something different?" the principal said. "Suppose I gave you some coins, and I told you that if you could show restraint and not spend them for a year, I would give you the same amount of coins again plus add a bonus one. A year later, you hadn't spent the coins, so I did as I promised, bringing your total to seven. How many coins did I give you originally?"

"Three," Dean said.

"Right," the principal said. "How did you get it?"

"Well," Dean said, "I thought if I gave the one coin back, I'd still have six. That would be two times the original. So, six divided by two is three."

"Perfect," the principal said. "The coins are just the variable x, given meaning."

"Wow!" Dean replied. "You make it so understandable. Why don't you teach math?"

"I used to," the principal replied, "but nobody likes a math teacher. Believe it or not, I found people dislike me less as a principal."

It would be nice to say that Dean did well in his math class after that, but he didn't. But he did start doing well in math in the principal's office. He ended up there almost every day and passed the math exams with the highest grades, later becoming an engineer. Dean always said that detention math was the best math class he ever had with the best teacher.

The Old Truck

I saw a friend of mine, Alex, driving a new pickup, and I was excited for him. But I was also somewhat surprised. I knew he loved his old truck, yet I realized I hadn't seen it in front of his house for a few days. I was happy that he had finally been able to focus clearly on how useless the old truck was so he could buy a new one.

Have you ever spent an inordinate, unreasonable amount of time on an inanimate object? I know I have. Usually, it's something I am sure I can fix myself. Recently, it has been an old tiller. It seems I just get one thing fixed on it and something else breaks down.

For Alex, the inanimate object he had spent all his time on was the old truck. I don't know why he was so attached to it. I don't think he even knew. Maybe in his youth, he had dreamed of owning one like it, and that dream had instilled itself in his subconscious. Whatever the reason was, he loved the truck.

But the truck had long ago outlived its usefulness. It backfired like the blast of a rifle shot, it smoked like an addict, and the gas mileage was measured in gallons per mile, not miles per gallon. It spent more time in pieces in Alex's yard than driving on the road. Almost every Saturday, and many evenings, Alex could be found tinkering on his truck.

"I don't know a lot about the cost of auto parts," Alex's wife told me, "but I think Alex might have been able to buy a new truck twice over with the money he's spent on that old truck."

"What parts has he put into it?" I asked.

"He started out by replacing the engine," she said. "It had been going through so much oil we would pull into the gas station and add two quarts of oil and top the gas tank with one quart of gas. The engine change took a year. And in putting the engine back in, somehow the wiring was destroyed. So, he had to replace all that. But the fuses weren't the right ones, so when the electrical system overcharged, it blew out all the lights. But he finally got it running, and do you know what I said to him when he did?"

"What?" I asked.

"I said, 'Alex, why don't you sell that old thing while it's running, and you can get some money for it?' But he said that was silly because after putting all the money into it for a new engine and new wiring, he wanted to get his money's worth out of driving it. Besides, he said it would be just as good as new."

"I saw him replace the engine," I said. "But I didn't see him drive it much after that."

"Of course not," Alex's wife replied, displaying her annoyance. "We hadn't driven a hundred miles on the new engine when the transmission went out. Do you know how much a transmission costs? We would have been further ahead selling the old hunk of metal for scrap."

Our conversation had been some time back, so when I saw Alex driving the new pickup, I was happy for them. I figured Alex had finally been able to break himself away from the old truck. I saw him at a community gathering and thought I would ask him about it.

"So, I see you got yourself a new pickup," I said.

"Oh, it's not ours," Alex replied. "We just borrowed it."

"Why did you borrow it?" I asked.

Before he could answer, another friend jumped into the conversation. "Alex, you know you should have sold that old truck when it was running."

"Now, don't you start," Alex said. "You sound like my wife."

I wondered what that had to do with Alex borrowing the new pickup, but I thought it might not be the best time to ask anymore. I also wondered what had happened to the old truck. But a little while later, I saw Alex and his wife go by in the new pickup. I smiled and waved, but they seemed intent on wherever they were going. A short time later, they came back towing the old truck. They parked it by their house, and Alex started working on it again.

I shook my head, smiled, and went back to work on my tiller.

Reason for Being Late

When eight-year-old Katherine walked into class, the teacher looked at the clock. It was almost noon. Few students came to school that late without a good reason.

"Well, Katherine," the teacher said, "would you like to tell us why you're so late?"

"A moose," Katherine replied.

"A moose?" the teacher asked, skeptically. "I can't just write 'a moose' as a reason on the late slip. The secretary will think I'm crazy. What about a moose?"

"Well, a moose wandered into our yard this morning," Katherine said. "The dogs decided to chase her. They chased her a distance down the road, but then she decided she had had enough. She turned around and chased them back to the shed that was just past the house."

"Okay," the teacher said. "But I don't see why that made you late."

"That was only the beginning," Katherine said. "When the moose turned to walk away, the dogs chased her again. Then, after they had gone a short distance, the moose turned and chased them back. The dogs hid in the shed, so the moose turned to walk away. But the dogs took off after her again. They went back and forth that way all morning. We watched it all through our window as we ate breakfast."

The teacher sighed, feeling that this story wasn't getting anywhere. "But what does that have to do with you being late for school?"

"Each time the dogs chased the moose, and the moose chased them back, the moose appeared to get a little bit madder. She ran after the dogs a little bit faster, and each time, she was closer to the dogs' tails by the time they reached the shed.

"After quite a bit of this, it was time for the bus to come, so we carefully checked outside to see if the coast was clear. We hadn't seen the dogs or the moose for about ten minutes. The last we time we saw them, the dogs were hot in pursuit of the moose as she headed over the hill across from our house.

"So, we made our way out to stand by the mailbox and wait for the bus. We had only been there a minute or two when the dogs came running back over the hill, with the moose almost on top of them. The dogs were whining as they ran. They seemed to know they weren't going to make it to the shed before the moose stomped them into compost.

"But then the dogs saw us, and they must have thought we could save them. They headed right for us. We didn't know what to do except to run, so we ran back to the house, screaming for Mom. Mom came out and saw us all heading for the front door, and she started screaming to scare the moose away, but it kept coming.

"We all ran into the house with the moose not too far behind. We ran into the bedroom, and Mom slammed the door behind us. We all made it in, the dogs, us, and Mom. After we caught our breath, Mom said she was sure a moose wouldn't follow us into the house, so she slowly opened the door to peek out. But the moose was right there in our living room.

"The moose snorted as if daring us to come out of the bedroom, so Mom quickly slammed the door again. Just about then, the bus started honking, and one of the dogs started barking. Then he bayed at the moose as if challenging her. Mom took a pillow and hit the dog across the face. But the barking apparently made the moose mad because she started stomping our living room floor, rocking the whole trailer house.

"Mom said if we could keep the dogs quiet for a while, the moose would probably leave. So, we all grabbed pillows, and the dogs seemed to sense it was better to stay quiet. Over the next few hours, Mom peeked out a few times, and the moose was still there. My brother said he thought maybe she planned to stay all winter and take control of the tv remote. But finally, when Mom peeked out, the moose was gone. Mom carefully went into the living room, looked through the window, and saw the moose in the yard. We stayed in the house and kept the dogs locked up and quiet in the bedroom until the moose left. Then Mom drove us to school."

The teacher looked at the line on the tardy paper that said, "Reason for tardy," paused momentarily, then simply wrote, "A moose."

Santa and a Christmas Wish

Okay, so I'm not your regular Santa, but I do enjoy visiting with people in that capacity. It started with my daughter. She was a music teacher in a local school district, and she was having a Christmas program in an attempt to earn money for her financially strapped program. She hoped to purchase instruments for children to play who could not otherwise afford to be in the band. She called and asked if I would be Santa.

I agreed, and my wife found a Santa suit in the want ads. I was soon outfitted for the part, but my temperament was questionable. The day came, and I ho-hoed my way into the gymnasium. I was soon surrounded by all ages, from babies who were placed on my lap, to middle-aged women plopping on my lap and saying, "Selfie!" as they snapped a picture. But parents and youth alike found I was not a usual Santa.

"I don't believe in you," one little eight-year-old girl said.

"That makes us even," I replied, "because I don't believe in you either."

"He's a mighty sassy Santa," the girl's mother said to the girl's grandma.

The shocked look on the little girl's face was priceless, but she quickly recovered.

"Can I pull your beard?" she asked.

"Of course," I replied, "as long as I can pull your hair."

Again, the shocked look on the little girl's face was good pay for doing this assignment.

"I don't think I like this Santa," the little girl's mother said. But the little girl hugged me and said, "I like you. All the other Santas are so unreal."

Next up were some teenagers. One boy, who was about sixteen, plopped on my lap. When I asked what he wanted for Christmas, he pointed at the girl behind him and said, "her."

"In your dreams!" the girl said to the boy.

I laughed at her spunk. "I'll hold him, and you slap him," I said to her.

The teenagers all laughed, including the boy on my lap and the girl he had mentioned.

"Well," the boy said, "if you can't get her for me, can you get me another girlfriend?"

"Look," I said, "Santa does magic. He doesn't do miracles."

All the teenagers laughed again, and one said, "Touché."

From then on, the teenagers asked for all sorts of crazy things just to see how I would respond, and many of them joined in the fun. The next boy asked me for an A in math.

I didn't even have to respond. The boy behind him did. "That would definitely be a miracle," the boy said. "And you heard what Santa said about the fact he doesn't do miracles."

All the other teens laughed. And so went the night. In the midst of all the teens were the small children, whom I loved to visit with. They had so much hope and excitement glowing in their little faces. But mostly, I noticed two small boys, both about six years old, hanging back, waiting patiently until all the others were done. Finally, when everyone else had gone, the two boys shyly came together, and one climbed on each knee.

"What would you like for Christmas?" I asked.

"I want my daddy to come home," each one said at almost the same time.

I looked at the two boys. One had beautiful brown skin, dark eyes, and black hair. The other was blonde with blue eyes and light skin.

"Are you two, um... related?" I asked.

They shook their heads. "Just friends," one replied.

"Tell me about your fathers," I said.

I learned that one boy's father had gone away, leaving his mother struggling to take care of herself and her son. The other boy's father was in the military and was deployed. The commonality of what they wanted most had brought them together as friends.

For the first time, I found myself without words. Finally, I said, "You know, your fathers may not be around this Christmas, but others, even some you may not know, love you."

They sat on my lap, and I talked to them for quite a while, even telling them a story or two. When they left, they seemed happier, and their mothers thanked me. But I didn't feel it needed to end there. I motioned my daughter over and pointed out the two families as they headed out the door. My daughter knew who they were, and after I told her the story, she said she knew some people who wanted to help families who had needs.

So that Christmas, two little boys and their families received an extra bag of presents on their doorsteps. And I learned that there is a little bit of Santa in all of us.

New Year's Commitments

Even though it had been a few years since I had been a scoutmaster, I always tried to go on campouts with the boys when an extra adult was needed. This mostly fell on the high adventure in the summer, which lasted most of a week. Each year, as we hiked miles into the wilderness or attempted steep mountain terrain, I felt the challenge of my age a little more. And each time, I made a mental commitment to get into better shape.

I missed a couple of years of high adventure due to other responsibilities, and when I was able to go again, there were some new scouts. We were camping at the base of Mount Borah, the highest peak in Idaho, facing the challenge of climbing it the next day. We had just finished dinner for the evening when one of the younger boys, Jason, mentioned that he wanted to play a game of old sow.

For those of you who have never played old sow, it's a game with about six to eight players, a hockey puck, clubs to pound the hockey puck, and everyone against everyone else. I doubt I need to say how this type of game plays out with a group of rambunctious boys, but I will mention that few ever go away from the game without a nice collection of bruises.

Jason started getting the game together, and a few of the boys his age agreed to play. But he really needed at least one more player. He went to all the older boys first, and all of them turned him down. He then started at the youngest leaders and worked his way up. I was the oldest leader by a good ten years, so after all the others had turned him down, I was the last one for him to ask.

He approached me with skepticism that I would accept. "Daris," he said, "I know you're old and out of shape, but we really need someone to play old sow with us."

He had me at the "old and out of shape" line.

"Get me a stick," I growled, "and prepare for a whippin'."

He excitedly ran back to the other boys and told them the news. They quickly found me a big club, and after I whittled it somewhat smooth, we were in business.

I might have been old and out of shape, but I had played some tough games of old sow. The boys soon learned that experience could make up for an overabundance of energy. I blocked their sticks and moved the puck with great expertise.

"Wow!" Jason said, "I've never seen anybody play like that."

By the time the game was over, I had earned their respect, even though I was gasping for air. I determined once more to get into better shape. The hike the next day only increased that resolve. Still, by the time the new year rolled around, I hadn't started an exercise routine. However, the thought of the high adventure only six months away made me recommit.

The days went by, and work and other challenges took priority. Before I knew it, we were on a high adventure again. This time, I was the scoutmaster. Our camp was at Bear Lake with lots of water activities. One of them included carrying our big paddle boards down the mountainside, spending a day on the lake, then carrying the paddleboards back up to the waiting trailer.

We carried the boards down in groups, two on each board, making multiple trips. We spent a long time on the lake, and it was past time to set up camp. As the boys started struggling up the mountain, two carrying a paddleboard, I decided we needed to hurry things up. I threw one on my shoulder and carried it up by myself. I even passed the boys. But when they finally caught up to me at the top, I was still struggling to catch my breath.

Jason looked at me and said, "You know, inside all that old fatness, you're actually pretty strong."

That was when I made a renewed commitment to get into shape again. I still plan to make that my new year's commitment—right after I finish off the last of the Christmas pie, so it doesn't go to waste.

Vacationing in Winter

It was cold in Idaho that year when we left for California for the Christmas break. The thermometer read fifteen below zero.

This vacation was going to be a big event for our children since we planned to take them to one of the big amusement parks. With the number of children we had, it pretty much required a reverse mortgage on our house to do something like that.

We couldn't afford to stay in hotels and pay the ticket prices, too, so we took our tent trailer with us. We probably looked crazy heading through Idaho pulling it. The snow on the side of the road was at least six feet high, and a family staying in a tent trailer in Idaho would raise questions about a person's mental stability. However, with it being Christmas break, our biggest concern was if there would be any spots in the California campgrounds, and if the amusement park would be so full we would have to wait in line more than ride the rides.

As we came down out of the mountains of Utah, and the snow faded into the deserts of Nevada, our two youngest children raised other concerns about there not being any snow for Santa's sled. We planned to spend Christmas with my in-laws in San Diego, and our smallest children were afraid Santa wouldn't be able to find us or land his sleigh there. We told them we let Santa know where we would be, and I said Santa's sleigh was equipped with wheels that he could put down when there was no snow for the sleigh. This seemed to satisfy them.

When we finally got to the campground, my wife and I went into the office to see if there was any space. When we asked about it, the clerk laughed.

"Honey," she said, "this is winter. Only those with good, warm motorhomes camp in the winter." Then she asked, "And what kind of motorhome do you have?"

"We don't," I replied. "We have a tent trailer."

"Are you plumb crazy!" she replied. "It's sixty degrees out there!"

I shrugged. "I've camped with my scouts at thirty-five degrees below zero before."

She looked at me like she thought I was making that one up, but she registered us into the campground. We were just leaving the office when I thought of something else.

"Do you have a pool?" I asked.

She nodded. "But it isn't heated."

"That's okay," I replied. "The river we swim in in the summers in Idaho is snowmelt coming off the mountain. It's probably only fifty degrees at its warmest."

That night, we had much of the campground to ourselves, and our children played a rousing game of Marco Polo in the pool. No one else came swimming. Oh, a few people saw us swimming and came and stuck a foot in, but then they quickly left. The clerk came to see what all the noise was about and went away shaking her head.

The next day at the amusement park was bright and sunny. The temperature was in the seventies, and the lines were long. Then, at about noon, clouds moved in, and it cooled off considerably. Soon, the temperature was down around sixty degrees. About half the people left, and most of the ones who stayed left briefly to bundle into coats.

My children's favorite rides were the water rides. These were in logs, or on six-person inner tubes riding down rapids. These rides pretty well emptied out. We could ride them, and when we got to the end, the lines were so short, we would be back on the ride in about five minutes. All in all, we had a really good time. But what I found was the most interesting part of our vacation was what my littlest daughter said about it. After we returned to Idaho, a neighbor asked her what she liked best about our vacation. Her answer surprised me.

"When we were at the amusement park," she said, "in the afternoon, people dressed their dogs in sweaters. It was so funny."

What made me smile about it was she thought they had done it strictly for our entertainment.

Home

This week, I helped my son as he moved his family across the country to a new home. He has a one-year-old daughter, and the whole episode reminded me of our first move after my wife, Donna, and I were married.

We, too, had a one-year-old daughter when we moved from the university where I received my bachelor's degree to where I would be going to graduate school. Celese was barely beginning to talk, and our small basement apartment was the only home she had ever known.

Because of our limited income, to save money, we did a twelve-hour rental for the moving truck. Donna took me to get the truck at eight o'clock in the morning, then she and I set to work packing it. We already had everything in boxes, and it was just a matter of fitting all our earthly belongings into it.

The whole time we were loading it, Celese was upset at seeing her toys, her bed, and all the other things that made it home to her being taken away. But when the truck was all packed, and we climbed into it to drive the two-and-a-half hours to our next apartment, she started to sob openly. She seemed to understand that we were leaving and not coming back. As I drove, Donna comforted Celese, and eventually, Celese fell asleep.

When we pulled up to our new apartment, already exhausted from loading everything, Donna and I started to unload. I brought in a few boxes, and Donna unpacked some of Celese's favorite toys trying to help her feel more secure in our new home. But instead, she was even more upset, apparently wondering why we were putting the things she loved in this strange place.

We finally finished unloading. I swept out the truck, put my bike in it, and headed on the road to take the truck back. I arrived back at the rental store barely before eight o'clock. I checked the truck in, then biked back to our old apartment. I busied myself cleaning and working to finish up all the things we weren't able to do before we left. At ten o'clock, my kind landlord stopped by.

He looked at me and shook his head. "You look absolutely exhausted. Are you planning to drive back to your family tonight?" When I nodded, he said, "You've done enough. You go ahead and go to them, and I will finish this another day."

Donna and I had talked about me staying overnight with my sister who lived near there, but I wanted to be back with my family. I struggled the whole drive to stay awake. But when I finally pulled into the driveway of the apartment building, I looked at the window, and Celese stood there, her little face pressed against the glass, watching for me. The tears were streaming down her face. As I came into the apartment, she ran to me, and I scooped her into my arms.

Donna gave me a hug. "I'm glad you came back and are safely here. Celese has cried the whole time you've been gone and refused to go to bed. I tried to cuddle her, but she wouldn't let me. She just kept going to a door and patting it, saying, 'Go home. Daddy.' I tried to tell her this was home, but it didn't help. Finally, I told her that you would be coming back, so for the last hour, she has stayed at that window watching for you."

I cuddled my sobbing daughter in my arms, and soon, her tears turned to sniffles and finally subsided completely. As I rocked her, her eyes started to flutter. Just before she fell asleep, she looked up at me and smiled, and said two words. "Home. Daddy." With that, she drifted off to sleep.

She never cried about going home after that. It seemed that even though she was very young, once the three of us were all together again, it was home, even if it was far from the little apartment she was familiar with.

She somehow understood what too often many of us forget: home is not so much a place; it is about being with those we love.

An Embarrassing Event

One of my scouts asked me about my most embarrassing moment. I could think of many, but because I had just been to a wrestling match, I thought of one that had to do with that sport.

The year before the particular embarrassing event, I had to run for my life from a pack of coyotes while trying to save a newborn calf and its mother. It was winter, with temperatures at about thirty degrees below zero. The cold and stress on my lungs helped bring on pneumonia to such an extent that I was in fairly critical condition for about two weeks.

After that, any time I stressed my lungs a lot, I would have trouble breathing. I struggled mildly through track that spring and football in the fall. But when it came to wrestling, I was really having trouble. Finally, my parents and my coach insisted that I see a doctor.

After many tests, the doctor told me I had some severe lung damage. He said the main problem was that the lung tissues were damaged to the point they were having a hard time staying moist like they needed. Whether the damage was caused by the overexertion while exposed to the freezing cold air or from the pneumonia, he wasn't sure. But he said the key was to be able to moisten them up before a physically demanding event.

He prescribed the use of an inhaler. He taught me how to put the nozzle in my mouth and pump a few shots of it while breathing the moisture into my lungs. The doctor told me it would not be against any kind of athletic rules because it had no steroids in it. He also told me to use it just before wrestling practice each day and before each match.

At the next practice, I explained to my coach what the doctor had said. My coach was concerned enough that every afternoon before practice, he would ask me if I had used the inhaler. But at the first match, neither he nor I thought about what taking some breaths from the inhaler might look like. Just before I stepped onto the mat, I took a couple of deep breaths from it as prescribed. The other coach saw what I did and immediately told the ref that I was taking drugs. The ref said he was going to disqualify me from the match.

My coach then told the ref that what I took was doctor prescribed, and if the ref disqualified me for it, he could lose his job. "You know very well that the rules allow an athlete to take doctor-prescribed medicine."

For about fifteen minutes, the whole gym was in an uproar with the opposing team wanting me disqualified and acting like they would lynch me. Fortunately, it was a home meet, and they and their fans were far outnumbered by ours. Finally, the ref decided that the best thing to do was to call the doctor who prescribed the medicine. It took about ten more minutes to get hold of him, and when the doctor explained that the medicine was nothing more than something to put moisture into my lungs, the ref told the opposing team what he had learned.

The opposing coach still demanded I be disqualified. So, the ref showed him the rules about doctor-prescribed medication and told him if he made one more remark about it, he would be removed from the gym.

By the time the match finally resumed, I was so embarrassed I just wanted to get it over with and be out of there. I pinned my opponent in under a minute, and that didn't help the other team feel any less that I had strength-enhancing drugs. But I had done the same thing every previous time we had met and had never had the medicine before.

When the wrestling meet was over, and we had won handily, the other team stormed away, still saying we cheated, even though we would have won even if they had won my match.

Our team met in the locker room afterward, and Coach sighed. "I'm glad that's over. But next time, Howard, bring your inhaler to the weigh-in to show the ref and the opposing team."

"I don't know, Coach," Lenny said. "The way Howard pinned that kid, maybe the rest of us should get inhalers."

Coach was in no mood to be teased and growled back his answer. "We'll just get all of you a spray bottle full of water, and you can just suck on that."

The Snow Challenge

Eight fourteen-your-old boys, two leaders, and six snowmobiles—what could possibly go wrong?

I was one of the fourteen-year-olds, and it was to be our January scout camping trip. We would snowmobile into a big, open meadow and set up camp Friday evening. We would spend the next day snowmobiling in the meadow. Then, an hour before dark, we would head for home.

All went as planned the first night. We set up camp and ate dinner. We went to bed early so we could get up at first light and have a full day riding the machines.

The next morning, there was only a glimmer of light in the east when we woke. By the time there was enough sunlight to ride without the machines' lights on, we were off racing across the meadow. After lots of riding, we moved to another fun event. We tied ropes fifty feet long onto the snow machines and tied the other ends to inner tubes.

"Howard," Rod said, "I bet you can't stay on that inner tube with me driving the snow machine."

I accepted his challenge and climbed on the inner tube like a cowboy climbing into a chute on the back of a bull. I grasped the rope securely with both of my glove-covered hands and lay down. Rod sat down on the snowmobile and gunned it forward.

Rod would bring the machine up to the fastest speed he could, about fifty miles per hour, then he would turn as sharply as he could without rolling the snow machine. This whipped me at about twice that speed in an arc across the snow. The snow crystals bit into the exposed areas of my face. I even rolled over a couple of times on the inner tube. But even while being dragged through the snow, I held on, determined to win the challenge.

The day was spent with everyone challenging each other to see if they could throw them off the inner tubes. When it was almost time to leave, only Rod and I had not been thrown off. Before heading back to where the snowmobile trailers were waiting, the other boys egged us on to see if one of us would be the ultimate champion.

Rod said he'd try to throw me first. For about twenty minutes, he rode at full throttle, crossing rough trails, turning at high speeds. The ice crystals cut into me to the point I felt they were surely drawing blood. But I held on, and finally, it was my turn to drive.

As he grabbed the rope, he grinned. "All right, Howard. Give me your best shot."

I, too, did the same as Rod had done. I pushed the machine to the limit across some of the roughest tracks and spun the machine in as fast and tight of circles as I could. But Rod held on no matter how hard I tried. I could see the sun sinking in the sky. Knowing my time was running out, I got a brilliant idea.

On the far side of the meadow was a ridge where the snow had drifted especially deep and thick. It had formed a wall of snow about eight feet high and around ten feet deep. It was also nearly vertical. I opened the throttle and headed for this wall of snow. I estimated the distance of the rope and the speed, and not far from the snow wall, I started the turn.

The rope whipped Rod toward the wall. I knew if I had estimated it right, he would hit the wall at peak speed, just as the rope went tight. It was almost perfect, and when the inner tube hit the wall, the g-force and the crash combined ripped Rod from the rope. But my fourteen-year-old brain didn't consider what would happen after that. The inertia shot Rod directly into the wall of snow like a human rocket. He disappeared right up to his boots. Suddenly, the thought went through my head that I had killed him.

The leaders and other boys must have thought so, too, because they came flying toward us on the snowmobiles. We dug around Rod's legs, then got a few of us on each leg and pulled him out. He was sputtering and spitting snow, but he was mostly fine. So much snow was rammed down his coveralls that he couldn't move, and we had to help pull them off of him and unpack the snow.

When we were sure he was okay, our leaders just sighed and looked at me, shaking their heads. Finally, the oldest one spoke.

"Sometimes, I wonder if fourteen-year-olds ever think at all where their actions will lead."

Refried Beans

My daughter, Celese, worked at a taco establishment. One of the things that annoyed her most was when boys came in and flirted crudely. Unfortunately, just such a group of boys had started coming in every evening and stayed until closing. The girls working there were getting fed up with the boys' sexist attitudes.

One evening just before the dinner rush, Celese, who was shift manager, made a frightening discovery. They had run out of refried beans. The workers checked everywhere to see if there were more. Many of the restaurant foods were quite impossible to make without them. Finally, Celese called the restaurant owner who didn't like being bothered at home.

When she told him the problem, he sighed. "I know we're out. We went through more than usual, and the shipment doesn't come in until tomorrow."

"What should we do?" Celese asked.

"Do two things," the owner replied. "To try and get people to buy chicken instead, put all chicken items at twenty-five percent off. If people still order bean items, you will have to use the instant refried beans. There are some twenty-five-pound bags in the southwest corner of the storage room. They aren't nearly as good, and they are quite old, so we ought to get rid of them, anyway. Heap them on to make the customers feel like they are getting a good measure."

Celese hung up the phone and told her coworkers what they needed to do.

"Instant?" Sheila said. "Those things taste okay, but they give a person more gas than a tanker truck, along with the runs if you eat too many."

"Well, we don't have much choice," Celese said.

Celese retrieved one of the bags of instant refried beans and read the instructions. It said, "Soak beans for fifteen minutes before heating."

She set a five-gallon bowl of them soaking, and it was just in time, because the dinner rush was starting. Most people ordered the on-sale chicken items, but a few ordered bean foods.

They were just getting through the dinner rush when, right on schedule, the annoying boys came in. The boys started in with their crude remarks, thinking they were flirty and funny. The girl working at the counter was new and was almost in tears when she came to get Celese.

"Some boys are asking for the manager," she said.

Celese knew who it must be, and she sighed and went to the front.

"Hey, hot Babe Manager," the lead boy said. "We know you love us and thought you might have some free food you wanted to give us."

Celese thought to herself that there was something free she wanted to give them as she doubled up her fists. Then Sheila pulled Celese aside.

"Why don't you give them some bean burritos?"

"But they are instant, and you said they give a person gas and the. . . "

Celese stopped as Sheila grinned and nodded. Celese realized what Sheila was saying.

Celese stepped back to the counter and smiled at the boy. "You are in luck. Because you are our most constant customers, tonight you get all the bean burritos you can eat for free."

"For free?" the boy said. "You must really love us, Blondie."

"If you only knew how much," Celese mumbled under her breath.

She got her crew busy hydrating beans and making bean burritos. During the evening, Celese figured each boy ate about a dozen. But then, they suddenly started looking very uncomfortable. Eventually, from one boy exploded a sound that made everyone stare and filled the restaurant with a smell that resembled something coming from an open tear gas canister. Soon, the boys were rushing to the bathroom. They left immediately after, which was good, because the smell had pretty much cleared the restaurant of paying customers and needed to be aired out.

However, the best part was that it was about a week before the much more humble boys came back. But still, Sheila hid the last bag of instant refried beans away just in case they were needed again.

A Timeout

My wife, Donna, and I were out buying items for our children and grandchildren when we ran into an old friend in the Valentine's Day aisle at the store. Mike, a very good man, had taught many of our children in school.

He smiled when he saw us and asked, "So, how many children do you have left at home?"

"Two," I replied. "All the others are off to college or married. How about you?"

"Oh, my wife and I have been empty nesters for a few years," he replied.

I knew he had around six children, so I said, "I bet it seems quiet around your house with all the children gone."

He shrugged slightly. "I guess it is. I kind of like it. In fact, I must have gotten used to it, because every time the grandchildren come to visit, I about go crazy from the noise."

"How many grandchildren do you have?" Donna asked.

"Fourteen. But the problem is, they are all under five. All my children got married within a couple of years of each other and started having children at the same time."

"Wow!" I said. "Fourteen under five!"

"I bet there's a lot of pandemonium in your house when they're all home," Donna said.

"That's kind of an understatement," Mike replied.

"In one of Daris's plays, a little girl calls family pandemonium 'happy noise,' " Donna said.

"Well, we have all fourteen at our house right now," Mike said, "and I think we have so much happy noise that I am about to check myself into a mental institution."

"So, what does your wife think about it?" Donna asked.

"She loves to have them all home, and I swear that with her, the more noise, the better. When I start to get tense, she tells me it's time for me to take a timeout."

"A timeout?" Donna asked.

"Yes," Mike replied. "She'll say, 'Mike, don't you have papers to grade or something?' Then I know that she's telling me to take a timeout."

"How does that work for you?" Donna asked.

"It actually works well. I leave all the noise behind and find something else to do until I am not so keyed up that I can once again deal with the commotion."

I had to smile at the idea of Mike having to have a timeout. He was one of our children's favorite junior high teachers. He taught science, and the children often did experiments in his class. But when a child got out of hand, Mike would have that child take a "timeout." That meant they were supposed to go do something away from the experiment that the other students were doing. The rambunctious student was allowed to read, draw, or do anything that was quiet. It just had to be something to give the child a little time alone to get themselves back together before joining the others again. The idea that what he used as a teacher for students was being used by his wife for him was what made me smile. Perhaps that was the reason he used it.

"What are all your grandchildren doing at home right now?" Donna asked.

"I'm not sure," Mike said. "They were being really noisy when I left."

I laughed. "Let me guess. You're in a timeout right now?"

Mike nodded. "You've got it. I thought I would make use of it to buy my grandchildren some Valentine's candy. Because, even if I need to take a timeout from them, I still want them to know I love them."

I nodded. Perhaps a timeout would be good for all of us now and then.

Vehicular Break-in

It had been a long day of work, and it was late and dark on a winter evening when I left my office. When I got to my little pickup, I found it covered with snow and ice. I unlocked it and started it so it would warm up while I scraped the windows. I chipped away the snow and ice and then stepped back to the pickup door, only to find it locked.

I realized that I was in a real predicament. My pickup was running, I had locked my keys, including my office keys, inside, and my colleagues were all gone, so I couldn't ask them for help. This was before the days of cell phones, so I didn't have anything with which to call home.

I thought about walking around campus to try to find some place from which I could call my wife, but I knew there weren't any public phones, and there was not likely anyone still at work. I also realized that if I did call my wife, she would have to come out on this dark, cold night and travel the twenty miles to come to my rescue.

As I pondered my options, I saw the small back window into the cab and remembered that I had opened it the previous night. I check and happily found that it was still unlocked. I climbed into the back of the pickup and pushed the window open. It was less than a foot on each side, wider than it was high, but I thought I could reach through it and pull the keys from the ignition. I stuck my arm through, but the pickup was an extended cab, and my hand was nowhere near the keys. I pushed my head through with my arm, and still my reach was more than a foot from the keys. To have any chance of reaching them, I had to get through to at least my waist.

I took off my coat and set it on the side of the truck, shivering in the below-zero temperature. I then stuck both arms through the window, which left little room for my head. By laying my head flat between my arms, I was barely able to get it through into the pickup. By wiggling and squirming, I was able to get my shoulders through, but that was as far as I could go. I could not get my midsection through the window. I was far enough in that the keys dangled at my fingertips, but I might as well have been a mile away. I could push in no further, and I knew trying was futile. It was time to give up on this plan.

I started to back out, but then my clothes hooked on the edge of the window. I tried to tuck them around me, but it was to no avail. No matter how I tried, I could not get out of the window. The cab was overly warm, and my top half was sweating even as my lower half was freezing. I struggled for around fifteen minutes to no avail, and I thought I was going to be stuck there until one of my colleagues found me the next morning. I thought it couldn't get any worse. At least that's what I thought until I saw the blue and red flashing lights pull up behind me.

A flashlight suddenly blinded me through the window. "All right," a voice commanded, "come out with your hands up!"

"If I could come out, don't you think I would have already?" I asked.

Another flashlight shown in from the other side. Then a smart-alecky voice spoke in a horrible English accent. "Holmes, I do say, I think he's stuck."

I almost said, "Great deduction, genius," but I refrained.

Eventually, they used a flat piece of metal to unlock the door. With one on the inside and one on the outside, they helped me get free. But then came the questions. They had received a report of someone trying to steal a pickup. What was I doing trying to break into it?

I told my story, and the fact it was locked and running was evidence in my favor. Eventually, they let me get the pickup registration and show them my I.D.

Just before they left, one officer said, "You should realize you're too. . ." He paused, then continued, "uh, big, to get through that window."

"Go ahead and say it," I said. "The word is fat."

He struggled to keep a straight face. "I didn't say that."

Then he and his partner laughed as they headed to their patrol car.

He didn't have to say it. I already knew.

The Garden Plot

Jenny was a farm girl living in a big city. She heard about an organization that allowed people to have a small garden plot for a nominal fee. She missed the joy of growing her own vegetables and the wonderful taste of fresh food, and she knew she could use the food to supplement her limited income. She soon had a small plot and was squeezing everything she could into it. She enjoyed taking the break from her busy life, and she enjoyed the people she associated with there. It wasn't long before she even became the organization's secretary.

She was there working in her garden one evening when a big, beautiful Mercedes pulled up. Everyone stopped and stared. It wasn't that they hadn't seen a Mercedes before; it's just no one who was part of the organization could afford one.

A man dressed in a three-piece business suit stepped from the car and asked who was in charge. Everyone pointed at Jenny, and he made his way toward her.

He stepped up and held out his hand. "Robert Stevens, the third."

Jenny held out her hand to shake his, but the minute he saw her soil-covered hands, he pulled his back.

"I came to see about getting a garden plot," Robert said.

By this time, all the other gardeners had joined Jenny and stood looking on curiously.

Jenny glanced once more at the Mercedes before turning back to Robert. "Why would you want a garden plot?" she asked.

The man sighed in annoyance, as if Jenny should just give him one and be done with it. "My doctor said I have too much stress in my life, and he said that if I don't do something about it, I am going to have a heart attack. He suggested I garden. I can pay whatever I need to."

"It just so happens we have one available," Jenny said. "The previous gardener passed away recently. It's ten dollars per month plus a forty-dollar tilling fee."

Robert pulled two one-hundred-dollar bills from his pocket and handed them to Jenny. "Keep the change," he said.

Robert left, and Jenny paid the man who did the tilling. Jenny was working in her garden again the next day when Robert returned. He was dressed in nice slacks and a white polo shirt. He brought many seed varieties with him, and everyone who was there came over to give their opinions on how he should plant them and to help. Before Robert left that evening, his garden had nice little rows with newly planted seeds in them, and his shirt was nearly brown.

Robert always came in a new white polo shirt. At first, he came every evening, and Jenny showed him how to sprinkle his little garden. He always impatiently asked why nothing was happening. Then one evening, Jenny showed him the little green shoots of radishes coming out of the ground. Soon, there were carrots, and before long, all the seeds were up. Robert was ecstatic.

Robert missed a few days, and when he came back and looked at his garden, he called Jenny over. "What are those?" he asked.

"Those would be weeds," Jenny replied.

"What? Who planted them in there?"

Jenny tried to explain that weed seeds can lie dormant in the ground or blow in, but they just grow on their own. Robert was skeptical, sure someone was out to get him. Jenny suggested Robert bring a hoe the next time he came, and she promised to show him how to weed.

The next time Robert came, he had a hoe, and Jenny showed him how to gently work the weeds from around the vegetables. But when Robert took over, he started whacking at them like he was taking an ax to a petrified log, cursing as he worked. When he finally finished, his little garden was spread all over, with few vegetable plants left in it.

He turned to Jenny, wiping the sweat on his now gray polo shirt. "I don't see how this is supposed to help my heart. You said the last man who had this garden died. What did he die of?"

Jenny tried not to smile from irony as she answered. "He died of a stress-induced heart attack."

Robert dropped his hoe, climbed in his Mercedes, and Jenny never saw him again.

The Skunk Skin

What does a person do with the skin of a skunk? Well, Rick decided that it could be used for a practical joke. He placed it on his doorstep, and he loved to watch people do a double-take when they came to his door. Some people would see it from a distance and not even come to his door. Rick saw that as a definite plus. Rick thought fewer interruptions in life was always good.

Another advantage was it kept door-to-door salesmen away. But it also kept away people that his family did want to visit, so he decided to hide it somewhat under a bench that was there. That meant most people were almost on top of it before they saw it. Some people would stumble and fall backward, almost tumbling off the steps before they realized it was not alive. But it made it so people at least got close enough to know it would not get them.

Rick had a lot of fun watching out his window and seeing how people reacted, but he had to admit that he had almost taken a backward tumble once or twice himself. He was the one who had put it there, but there were times when he came to his own door while deep in thought, only to be startled into the present by the black and white fur sticking out from under the bench.

There was another advantage that Rick had found. Even though the skunk skin had long ago lost any scent it may have carried to human senses, it tended to deter wild animals from coming near. Rick found that he could put his cats' food bowl on the doorstep near the skunk skin, and wild animals didn't come around as much to eat the cat food.

Of course, at first, even his cats tended to shy away. But after some time, his own cats got used to it. He could put out some food, and his cats would come running. He was spending about half as much on cat food as before, and his cats were still fatter.

Word got around the community about the skunk skin, and soon everyone knew about it. People talked about it and joked about it. Still, even knowing it was there and that it was not alive, people approached Rick's door cautiously.

"Why do you keep that old thing around?" Rick's wife asked him one day.

"Give me one good reason not to," Rick said.

His wife's reasons were nonfunctional—things like the skin was old and ugly.

"Do you want me to bring it into the house to wash it and spruce it up?" Rick asked.

His wife said it would be the last conscious thing he ever did if she found that in her bathroom. And so, they compromised with Rick keeping it on the porch and never bringing it into the house.

Rick had had the skunk skin for over a year, and people in the community had quit talking about it. It was old news now. It didn't even catch Rick's attention anymore, even when he was deep in thought. He didn't even notice it was there.

But then one day, the word around the community was that the skunk skin was gone. No one knew for sure that it was, and no one knew why. But someone had heard something had happened. At church the next day, curious community members watched for Rick to come so they could find out the details. But Rick didn't come to church. However, his wife and children did, so people gathered around to hear the tale.

"Well, Rick came home yesterday," his wife said, "and he walked up on the porch as usual. Nothing seemed out of the ordinary to him until, suddenly, the skunk skin turned its back end toward him and put its tail in the air."

That was when Rick realized there was one animal that a skunk skin didn't scare away from eating out of the cat dish—another skunk.

No one except Rick's family saw him for a week or two. His wife said it was because he was feeling "scent-sitive about the odor-deal" he had been through.

A Check We Can't Cash

One of the jobs that I have as scoutmaster is to help teach the boys about serving others. Winter is good for that. There are always people who need wood chopped or hauled, and in a winter like this one, there is lots of snow to shovel.

One winter, we were receiving more requests for snow shoveling than my troop could keep up with. The moisture was coming down as slush and freezing solid on everything it touched. It was not only heavy, but it locked itself solidly to any surface. It had to be chipped off of roofs. Many farm buildings were caving in before they could be cleared.

One Sunday, while I was standing in the foyer at church, one of our community members walked in. Harry was covered in scrapes, bruises, and bandages. Both eyes were black. He didn't look good at all.

"Harry, what happened to you?" Bart asked.

Harry looked a little sheepish as he answered. "Well, the snow was building up on my shed, and I realized there were two problems with it. First, the weight was making the rafters bow, and secondly, the ice must have pushed open some of the tin, because water was dripping inside. I decided that I would get up on the roof and shovel off the snow and screw the tin down.

"I found my ladder, got my drill and shovel, and climbed up to the roof. I found the ice was much harder to break off than I thought it would be. I decided to get some off the edges to take off some weight, then I'd just cut a section up along where the roof was leaking so I could tighten the tin down. I was able to get the ice off the edges of the roof okay by moving along them and chipping at the ice while standing on the ladder, but cutting a path up the section of the roof where it was leaking was a lot harder.

"I eventually got a path cut through the ice, but the exertion made me gasp for air. I had just finished taking off enough ice so I could put the screws into the roof, and I was reaching for the drill when I suddenly felt dizzy. The next thing I knew, I was waking up on the ground, almost frozen to death. I have no idea how long I lay there, but it was getting dark."

"As banged up as you are, that must have been quite a fall," Ben said.

Harry shook his head. "That wasn't where I actually got really hurt. Oh, I was a little shook up and had a few bruises, but the thought of not even remembering what had happened was what bothered me the most. I got up and was really stiff and sore, and I struggled to walk to the house. I realized I should get some help to finish the job. But that was when I realized I had left the drill up on the roof."

Harry grinned in embarrassment, and we grinned, too. Every one of us grew up on a farm, and we all had a strong independent streak.

"In the meantime," Harry continued, "while I lay there, the moisture had frozen on the tin I had cleared. I stepped on the tin and had just reached out and touched the drill when I slipped. I do remember that fall as I came flailing off the roof. I was even still awake after I landed, and I immediately sat up. But then something hit me on the head. It was probably an hour or two later when I woke up, and the drill was laying by my face."

We were all glad Harry was all right. But the men couldn't help but give some good-natured teasing.

"That's one thing about it," Bart said. "A person never has to worry about falling off a roof because the ground is always there to catch him."

"I don't mind the fall," Ben said. "It's the sudden stop at the end that I hate."

Harry smiled at their teasing. "You know what I hate?" he said. "I hate getting old and having my mind write checks that my body can't cash."

New Technology

Cell phones were new, and the university made me carry one because I was the director of internet systems. They wanted to be able to get hold of me if something went wrong, which, with the internet in its infancy, it often did. Messages from my office phone were also routed to my cell phone and beeped me at the most inconvenient times. Sometimes, technology is so annoying.

Shandy's messages always beeped me at the worst times of all. Every time I had a test in my class, Shandy had some emergency come up. She would call and leave a message on my phone just before the test closed. For the first exam, my phone beeped just as I was trying to get my young children asleep. I picked up the phone and hit the play button.

Shandy's voice came on, and she was breathing hard. "Hello, Professor Howard. This is Shandy. My friends and I are at a park forty miles from campus, and someone in our group broke her arm. I ran to this payphone to call for medical help, and after I called them, I realized I should call you to let you know I won't make it back to campus in time to take the test. I hope you will let me take it tomorrow."

This was always a tough spot to be in. The student may or may not be telling the truth. I tended to err on the side of trust, so the next day I called the testing center and gave them the information needed to let Shandy take the test. I hoped that would be the last time, but when the second test came, there was a similar phone call. My phone beeped in the middle of an important meeting. Few others had cell phones, and everyone stared at me.

It was another call from Shandy. "Hello, Professor Howard. This is Shandy. I was coming home with some friends from a game about ninety miles from campus when we came upon a wreck. We helped the people get out before the car caught fire and treated them for shock until paramedics arrived. Afterward, we pulled into this gas station so I could call you. There is no way I can make it all the way back to campus in time for the test. I hope you will let me take it tomorrow."

Things didn't quite add up, but I had no proof to the contrary, so I called the test permission into the testing center. But then I called the Honor Office and asked them if they had received any concerns about Shandy. They said they had, but nothing that anyone could prove.

Two more tests had the same thing happen. My phone beeped at inconvenient times, and Shandy had had an emergency. But I was getting more suspicious. Still, I couldn't prove anything, so I called the testing center for her permissions.

Then, one day, there was a knock on my office door. I opened it, and there stood a man holding two phones. "We have upgraded the phone system on campus, and everyone is getting new office phones," he said. "You also get a new cell phone."

"What's wrong with my old phones?" I asked.

"I don't really know," he answered. "But apparently, they don't work well with the new equipment."

He set up my office phone, handed me the new cell phone, and left a small brochure on how to use the new features. I put the small brochure in my wallet. I didn't have time to deal with new technology, and I knew how to use a phone. But then came the day after the next test closed. My phone beeped while I was on a date with my wife. I was annoyed when I had to use the brochure to figure out how to get the message.

It was Shandy again. "Hi, Professor Howard. This is Shandy . . . "

Her message was the same as usual. She said she was two hours away from campus and had had an emergency. When she finished speaking, I was just about to hang up when a computer-generated voice came on. "This call originated from McKay Library extension 7042."

I paused, somewhat stunned. Shandy had called me from on campus, and now I knew for sure she wasn't really miles away.

Maybe technology was not so annoying after all.

The Ultimatum

My wife and my children are all very talented. They all play the piano, and most play multiple other instruments. My musical talent is limited to playing the radio. For those who know my brothers and sister and my parents, my lack of musical talent may come as a surprise. All my siblings are quite talented, especially on the piano. Many of them play for church and community events. My mother taught piano to hundreds of people over the years. So, how could one of her sons end up so lacking in this area?

As a boy growing up, there were cows to milk morning and night, plus lots of other chores to do. There was also only one piano, and I had six brothers and three sisters. Along with our practice, my mother taught piano lessons almost every evening after school and on Saturdays, too. That meant the piano had little chance to rest before the next person was playing. My parents worked out a tight schedule for my brothers, sisters, and me to practice piano.

The boys in the family were expected to start learning the piano by the time we were five, the same age we started doing farm chores. Because there were so many chores to do after school, and Mom was teaching her students piano, my brothers and I had to trade off mornings doing chores with mornings of piano practice.

Of all the people that my mother tried to teach, I was surely the one who tried her patience the most. When it was my morning to practice piano, my mother would get me started then leave to do her own work. But the minute she walked out of the room, my attention would turn to anything but the little dots and lines on the page. It wouldn't be long before I would hear her call, "I can't hear any piano playing!"

I would jump back up on the bench and play for a minute or two, only to be drawn quickly away by something more interesting. My parents tried bribes, threats, and just about anything they could to get me to practice, but it seemed so boring to me. By the time I was eleven, I was able to play the simplest of hymns, but my mother seemed to doubt whether she could keep my attention at it long enough to push me much further. After playing the same piece for recital two years in a row, with no new skill and the only difference being a little liberal flair on my part, my mother decided something had to be done.

One night, I overheard my parents talking about what they could do to get me motivated to really practice. My mother told my father that she just didn't know what more she could do.

My father chuckled a little. "You just leave it to me. You know how I have motivated all the other boys."

"Are you sure it will work with him?" my mother asked, the doubt prominent in her voice.

My father laughed. "It has worked on every one of them. I'll just wait for the right day." I wondered what day that would be.

One morning I woke up and the windows were covered with frost. The bedroom I slept in on the north of the house was so cold, my breath came out in steam as I climbed out of bed. It was my morning to practice, so after breakfast, I reluctantly, but dutifully, sat down at the piano. That was when my father came to me.

"Son, your mother says you don't concentrate on your piano practice. Well, it's forty degrees below zero outside. You can either sit in here in a warm house and diligently practice piano like your mother wants, or you can forget all about practicing the piano and get outside and do chores."

I couldn't believe he was giving me a choice. He never had before. I felt so happy. "Thanks, Dad," I said.

I got up off that bench, put on my work clothes, and went outside. And I never looked back at piano practice again. It wasn't until years later, when I thought about that experience and the shocked look on my father's face, that I realized that was not the outcome he had expected.

But that is why all my siblings play the piano so well and I don't.

A Change in Personality

My roommate, David, was dating a girl named Annie. She was beautiful, with blonde hair that hung down past her shoulders, and she had big blue eyes. But what made her especially beautiful was her kindness. David would invite her to join us in games of UNO. She never got upset when she lost, and she was always gracious when she won.

David would often invite Annie over to our apartment to eat with him. If any one of us were eating at the same time, Annie would suggest we pool our food and eat together. It was fun because it brought us all together and made us better friends. It was especially good for guys like me who usually ate alone.

One day as I was heading home, I ran into David. "Hey, Daris," David said. "Would you do me a favor? I have some things to do, and Annie is coming over to our apartment. I was wondering if you would mind visiting with her until I can get back?"

I thought that it was a strange request. She was his girlfriend, and I had never visited with her without him there.

"Uh, yeah," I said. "I'd be happy to visit with her."

"Thanks," David said. "Oh, and by the way, she might have gotten a haircut, so compliment her on that. If she's sensitive or upset, just visit with her and help her feel better."

He left, and I walked slowly to our apartment. I had never seen Annie sensitive or upset. She was always calm and positive, and she raised the spirits of those around her.

It was my day to do the dishes, so when I got to our apartment, I got started. I filled one sink with soapy wash water, put in the dishes, and had just stuck my hands into the water when there was a knock at the door. I turned, and through the window, I could see Annie.

"Come in," I called.

When she walked in, I was shocked to see her dressed strangely, and her long, beautiful hair was in a pixie cut. David had mentioned a haircut, but I was still shocked to see her hair so short.

When the shock wore off, I said, "Hi, Annie."

She glared at me. "What did you say?"

Taken aback by her sudden anger, I stuttered, "I . . . I just said hi."

"Yeah, right," she said sarcastically.

Not knowing what else to say, I said, "Your hair is cute."

"Cute!" she said in a tone that made me shutter. "Cute! You call my hair cute?"

I thought maybe she liked it better long, so I said, "Oh, it was also beautiful long, and I like it that way, too."

"So, my hair was beautiful long, but it's only cute when it's short?"

"Are you upset about something?" I asked.

"What makes you think I'm upset, and what business is it of yours, anyway?" she asked.

I tried to be nice and say anything I could to appease her, but she just grew angrier and angrier. Finally, she was up almost in my face. She scooped water out of the sink, splashed it all over me, and stormed out. I thought about how disappointed David was going to be in me that I had made Annie angry.

Not too long after that, David walked in. "David, I'm sorry," I said. "I made Annie angry, and I just made things worse when I tried to . . . "

I stopped. Annie walked in behind David. Her hair was long and beautiful, and she was dressed normally.

I was shocked. "But, Annie, your hair is long and beautiful, and your clothes are nice!"

"Thank you," Annie said sweetly.

"Did you like Angela?" David said with a laugh.

Annie turned to him. "Oh, David, you didn't?"

I was still in shock. "You're twins?"

"Triplets, actually," Annie said. "Amy and I try to look alike, but Angela gets mad when someone mistakes her for one of us. I try to warn my friends before they meet her. You didn't call her Annie, did you?"

I nodded.

David laughed again and said, "April Fools on you, my friend."

Sunk Boats

    My daughter and her family recently moved to Alabama from California. They have realized there are quite a few differences between the two areas. First, in California, they lived in Death Valley, and in Alabama, they live in a lush area with lots of rainfall. This has translated into a great difference in the plant and animal life around them.

    Another thing that Celese and her husband, Jimmy, have learned is the prices of the homes in Alabama are much lower. The home they purchased in Alabama would have cost them nearly four times as much in California. It also came with a couple of acres of land.

    Another big difference was there were no rivers or streams where they lived in Death Valley, so they were surprised to see how many properties had some type of waterway running through them. Celese couldn't believe the low price on one home they looked at. When they walked across the property, they found it went right down to the edge of a slow-moving river. Property like this in California would probably cost around thirty times the price being asked for this one. In fact, property with a river running along it would have been almost impossible to find in the area of California they had moved from.

    "How come the price is so low on this place?" Celese asked.

    "Two reasons," the realtor said. "The first reason is snakes."

    This excited Jimmy. Snakes fascinated him. He had owned a boa constrictor when they lived in California, but he had to give it away when they moved.

    "What kind of snakes?" Jimmy asked.

    "Water moccasins and brown snakes," the realtor replied.

    The thought of snakes made them forget to ask any more questions—for Celese because of the nervousness, and for Jimmy because of excitement. However, Jimmy was not familiar with water moccasins, so he decided to read more about them.

Celese and Jimmy continued to look at other houses, and in the evening, Jimmy looked up water moccasins and learned that they mostly only live in the southeast part of the United States. Jimmy was excited to find out more and talked Celese into going back to look at the property again.

As they walked along the river, Celese remembered a question she had from the first time on the property.

"You said there were two reasons the property was so cheap. You said one reason was snakes. What was the second?"

The realtor smiled. "Sunk boats."

"Sunk boats?" Celese questioned. "How did they sink?"

"Well, most people are quite afraid of water moccasins," the realtor said. "This area is one with a reputation for them, so people come here to hunt them. In actuality, there really aren't that many here. Mostly there are brown snakes, which look like water moccasins but aren't poisonous. People will float down the river and shoot at the snakes."

"But how does that cause the boats to sink?" Jimmy asked.

"People floating down the river will see a snake in a tree and shoot it. Water moccasins don't really climb trees, but brown snakes do, so the hunters are really shooting brown snakes."

"But that still doesn't tell us how the boats sink," Celese said.

"Quite often the snakes fall out of the trees into the boat," the realtor replied.

"But surely a snake falling into a boat wouldn't sink it," Jimmy said.

"It would if the person in the boat thinks it's a water moccasin, panics, and shoots it after it lands in the boat."

A Professional Job

I was a young, married college student. My wife and I had one small daughter, and every day after school, I went to the job board on campus to find work to earn money for my little family. People called in jobs they needed filled, and the secretary posted them on the job board. It was always minimum wage, $3.35 an hour, and temporary, so money was tight.

Winter was an especially hard time to find work, but in the summer, I could often find landscaping jobs. It was backbreaking work laying sod, moving rocks, and digging trenches. Few people wanted it, but I learned every aspect of it I could so I would be more valuable.

One spring afternoon, after checking the board for a few days without success, I visited with the secretary. I told her I desperately needed some work. She asked me what skills I had, and she wrote them down, along with my phone number. I told her I was willing to do anything.

At four o'clock the next morning, my phone rang. I groggily answered it.

"Hello," the man on the phone said. "The employment secretary, who is a friend of mine, gave me your number. I need someone to do the sprinklers for landscaping. Can you help me?"

"Sure," I replied. "When do you want me there?"

"Right now," the man replied.

Luckily it was Friday, and I had no classes. I was at the man's house by four-thirty. He told me his name was Wally. The landscaping on his new home was being done by the high school horticulture class as training for the students.

"But the problem is," Wally said, "the sod and the students are coming at eight o'clock this morning, and the landscaping instructor had a medical emergency and hasn't been able to finish the water system. Can you do it?"

I knew that if I had to dig all the trenches, it would be impossible. But when he shown his flashlight on his yard, I could see most of the trenches were already dug.

Handing me a schematic of the water system, he said, "I have no clue what this means."

I looked at the drawings and compared them to what was already done. "I think if I get busy, I can have enough done to keep ahead of the students laying sod," I said.

He handed me his flashlight, and I started laying pipe in the trenches. Using a level, I made sure there was some slant to the drain fittings so the pipes would drain for winter. I left openings at every spot where a sprinkler would go and worked quickly but carefully.

By the time the sod and the students came, the front lawn was ready. I showed them how to lay the sod and where to leave pieces out of the place where the sprinklers would go, and then I went to the backyard. There were more trenches to dig there, and that slowed me down. I also had to keep checking on the students and directing them. Still, as the sod started moving around to the backyard, I was able to keep ahead of them, but just barely. By the time it was getting dark, I had one thirty-foot trench still to dig, so I had the students lay the sod in stacks along it.

After the students left, I worked until past midnight and had all the sod in place except where the sprinklers went. I told Wally I'd be back first thing in the morning. I was back by five o'clock, and there was just enough daylight to work. I worked all day, and after a few tests and a few fixes, at just after midnight, I turned on the sprinkler system, and it worked flawlessly.

Wally smiled. "You've done well."

I was filthy, so I sat on the front step while he wrote me a check. In my head, I multiplied the thirty-nine hours for the two days times three-fifty and considered how much we needed the money. But when he handed me the check, I gasped. He had paid me ten dollars per hour. When I told him I thought he had overpaid me, he shook his head.

"You came at four in the morning and worked past midnight both days. You're as good as any professional landscaper I've seen, and you should receive a professional's wage."

I thanked him, and then he said, "And I have another week's worth of work you can do if you'd like. But it only pays five dollars per hour."

I smiled and said I'd be back first thing the next week.

As I drove home, as sore and tired as I was, it felt good to know I had done a professional job.

Bad Brakes

I first met Wally after he called me at four in the morning to put in his yard-watering system before the sod came that same day. He liked my work and hired me for another month. He had a new house, so he wanted help fixing up his old house so it would sell. It was hard work. I dug and hauled dirt, cut down trees, trimmed bushes, and did lots of other physical labor. I would always go home exhausted but grateful for the much-needed income.

Besides the fact Wally liked my work, I think he hired me because I owned a small pickup truck. Wally had nothing but a car, so he would pay me extra to haul stuff for him. I hauled some things to his new house, hauled some things to a second-hand store, and hauled some things to the dump. I took at least one load somewhere every day.

One day, I was busy trimming a hedge when Wally came to me.

"Daris, would you mind if I borrowed your truck?" he asked. "There's a couch my wife bought at the store, and I need to go get it."

"I'm okay with you using it, Wally," I said. "But there are two problems. It has a standard transmission, and the brakes are bad. I was planning to get the brakes fixed as soon as I had enough money."

Wally laughed. "I'm good with standards, and the brakes couldn't be that bad. I see you drive it over here every day, and you seem to stop okay."

"But do you see how I stop?" I asked. "I gear it down coming to a stoplight and try to coast until the light changes. If I have to come to a full stop, I shut off the key and kill the engine. Shutting off the engine is also how I stop in front of your house."

"But when you back into my yard to load stuff, you don't have a problem."

"That's because it's uphill," I replied.

He seemed to think I was exaggerating and assured me that he could do it, so I handed him the keys.

But I was not exaggerating. On downhill roads, the brakes wouldn't slow me down at all. I put it in first gear to keep my speed down. Other cars would pass me and honk.

As time went by and Wally didn't come back, I began to worry. I thought for sure he'd been killed, and it was my fault. But finally, I heard my pickup coming, chugging along in first gear. I felt better, sure Wally had figured it out. But when he pulled up, there was no couch. When he climbed out, he was breathing hard.

"Where's the couch?" I asked.

"Couch?" he said, almost yelling. "I didn't get anywhere near the furniture store! I only got to the first traffic light at the end of this street!"

"What happened?" I asked.

"I'll tell you what happened! Nothing! That's what happened when I pushed on the brakes! Nothing!"

"I told you the brakes were bad."

"Bad! They're nonexistent! I'm coming to the light, and I push on them. I don't even slow. I panic and swing the wheel to the right and go up on the sidewalk. I'm pumping the brakes for all I'm worth, but nothing is happening. I'm bearing down on people, so I lay on the horn. People are scrambling and dodging out of the way. Finally, the sidewalk narrows, and the wheels on one side go off, and the bottom of the pickup drags along the curb, bringing me to a stop. Then everyone starts yelling at me, and the police come and give me a warning."

"At least it was just a warning," I said.

"Yeah, well, now I'm giving it to you." Wally handed me the warning, and then wrote me a check. "And I'm also giving you an advance on your pay. You stop work right now and get those brakes fixed!"

I thanked him and did as he said. When I got back, I held out the keys. "Do you want to take it and go get the couch, now?" I asked.

"Not a chance. I lost ten years off my life the last time I drove it. You go get the couch, and I'll be here waiting for you when you get back."

Wally never did ask to drive my pickup again.

Feeling Useful

Have you ever had reason to wonder how useful you are? Recently, one of my daughters came home, saw me, and asked if I had suddenly gotten gray. I had to admit it was because I hadn't used Grecian in a while. With that grayness, some people think I can't do anything, and I feel old and useless.

A case in point occurred Monday. My daughter, Elliana, plays the harp. She's only sixteen but is very professional. She has played for weddings, Christmas gatherings, and even been the lead act for well-known musicians. Recently, a famous musician's staff posted that he was looking for some harpists to play in a music video. Donna, my wife, thought this would be a great opportunity for Elliana. Elliana loves the musician's music, so she was excited.

The video shoot was less than a week away, so Donna quickly applied. Three days later, Elliana was accepted, and early on Monday morning, we headed to Utah.

We got there early in the afternoon, and there was a lot to be done before the videotaping at three o'clock. The girls had to get on makeup, have their hair braided, and make sure all their clothing was just right. For most of it, I was the only dad there, and I felt useless. I asked if there was anything I could do, and the answer was pretty much for me to just stay out of the way.

The makeup took about two hours. Finally, it was time to move the harps into position. That was when we learned something interesting. The video shoot was to be in a dry water fountain, and the harps were to be lined up around the inside of the fountain. This posed a problem since the wall was about eighteen inches tall. At the thought of their harps being picked up a couple of feet and lifted over the wall into the fountain, looks of horror showed on the faces of the harpists and their mothers. Also, the film crew knew next to nothing about moving harps.

One girl had a small harp, and I asked the mother if she wanted me to lift it over the wall. She knew that there are certain ways to lift a harp because there are parts that should not be stressed. "Have you ever lifted a harp before?" she asked.

"I carried my daughter's full-size concert harp everywhere for years," I said.

She reluctantly agreed. I told two of the men from the film crew to get inside the fountain. I picked up the harp, keeping it upright, and handed it across the wall to them. They carefully set it down.

"That's fine with a small harp," one mother said. "But what about a full-size concert harp?"

She was not about to let me demonstrate with hers, so I got our own. Because of the brand it was, it was probably the heaviest model there. I had the men get into position, and I carefully lifted the harp up and over the wall to them. I was grateful I had been doing muscle-building exercises in an attempt to lose weight, because lifting that harp took all the strength I had.

The mother then turned to me and said, "You can lift mine, too."

I lifted her harp over, and the two men set it down.

"How many harps are there?" the film crew director asked.

"Around twenty-four," someone replied.

Having lifted the two big ones over, I gained the trust of the other mothers and started lifting each harp over to two of the film crew. There were twenty-six harps, and I was exhausted after that workout.

The film crew tested their big, heavy cameras, putting them on a cart to roll around as they filmed. But the round brick pavers caused the cameras to jiggle. They tried wagons and other carts with the same result. Finally, they just had to carry the cameras. But the film crew tired fast and could only work for about thirty seconds before playing tag and passing their camera to another crewman. We watched as they shot take after take until I could see their arms shaking from exhaustion. Finally, it was all done.

I figured after my first workout lifting harps, I would just do my own. It was all I could do to get a couple of film crew guys to take it on the outside of the fountain. I then realized all the mothers were waiting for me to lift theirs, too. I lifted every harp over, and the tired film crew traded off lifting them down. When I finished the last one, my arms were shaking from exhaustion.

I felt good when the film crew leader, only half-joking talking about me, said to his crew, "I ought to fire half of you and hire him. He lifted every harp by himself."

That made me feel good until he said, "And wow, he's old!"

Glad to Come Home

My daughter was in her mid-teens—those years when young people think their parents don't know too much. She chafed at the requirements of home, having to do chores, having a set time for bed, and eating what everyone else in the family ate instead of getting to choose for herself. She also felt that with all her siblings, there were just too many people with too many personalities to deal with. She often told us she couldn't wait to get away from home.

"Maybe I could find another place to live for the summer," she said.

"Like where?" I asked.

"I don't know," she replied. "Maybe I could go stay with Grandma. Maybe I could help her with her garden. It would give me a chance to get away from home."

The grandma she was talking about was my mother, and I was wondering if my daughter really knew what she would be getting herself into. My mother is a no-nonsense woman. As I thought about it, I wondered if that might be just what my daughter needed. I decided to talk to my brother. When I told him about what my daughter wanted, he laughed.

"One of my daughters got sick of everything at home and pushed us to let her go stay with her grandma, too," he said. "We finally let her."

"How did it go?" I asked.

"You know Mom," he said. "Life is about work and getting things done. Just because someone is staying with her doesn't mean that she has time to sit around and visit. It just means she has more help to get the things done she needs to get done."

My brother said that for a day or two, his daughter didn't say too much about it. But then, on day three, she let him know that she wanted to come home.

He told me his daughter said, "Grandma just keeps me working all the time. Coming home will be like going on a vacation."

"How long did she end up staying there?" I asked.

"She made it almost four days," my brother said. "But on the day she called to come home, she said she had been assigned to pick the thorny gooseberries, and that was the last straw."

I laughed. I love gooseberry pie, but picking the thorny things is one of the greatest trials of life. After visiting with my brother, my wife and I decided to let our daughter go stay with her grandmother. It was early spring, so there were not any berries to pick. But I knew my mother would find something to keep my daughter busy.

After almost a week had gone by, my daughter called and said she was ready to come home. When I picked her up, I asked her how it went.

"Oh, it was okay," she said.

"Just okay?" I asked. "What did you do?"

"The real question is what didn't I do?" she replied. "I cleaned out raspberries until my arms were all scratched up. I weeded, dug grass out of the garden, mowed the lawn, and trimmed the trees. And to top it off, today I had to clean dead branches out of the gooseberries. I think their thorns are about an inch long!"

I smiled. Those were some of the things I did when I was young. I appreciated my mother teaching my daughter to work. The next time I visited with my mother, I mentioned it.

She just shrugged. "I don't expect anything from your children that I don't expect from anyone else. I don't run a hotel, you know. If someone comes to visit, they are only guests for three days, and then they're family and have to pitch in. But in the case of your children, they are already family and should pitch in from the beginning."

My mother has now sold her farm, so my children won't be going there anymore, but on this Mothers' Day, I am grateful for a mother who helped teach my children how to work just as she and my father taught me.

Getting Tomatoes to Grow

✦

My cousin Becky loves gardening about as much as I do. We often compare notes on what works and what doesn't.

"How do you do on your tomatoes?" she asked.

"Oh, I do okay," I said.

"Do you do anything special?"

"Not really," I replied. "I do usually plant them in tires, so the tires heat up during the day and keep the tomatoes warm at night."

"Do you get a big crop?" Becky asked.

"I get an okay crop," I replied. "My biggest problem is I get them going well, I keep them weeded for about half the summer, but then everything hits at once. As a scoutmaster, I have scout camps, then the berries need picking, and the peas need shelling. The tomatoes grow weedy. They still produce well, but not as well as they could."

"Do you ever talk to your tomatoes?" she asked.

"Not intentionally," I replied. "Why do you ask?"

"As a girl growing up, my mother would swear that plants did better if you talked to them and praised them. I keep my tomatoes weeded, watered, and I talk to them."

"What do you say to them?" I asked.

"I tell them they are very good tomatoes, and that I love them. I also tell them, thank you for giving me food. But they still don't produce very well. Everything they give me is green and undersized."

"Do you fertilize them?" I asked.

"Yes. I get a load of fertilizer from the dairy farm that is just down the road."

"Maybe that's the problem," I said.

"What?" she asked.

"You tell them how beautiful and wonderful they are, then you dump a load of cow poop all over them. I think the problem is that after you tell them all those wonderful things, and then do that to them, they don't believe a word you say."

"Don't you use manure on yours?" Becky asked.

"Sure," I teased. "But I don't go extolling all the plants' virtues before I douse them in it. I just do it."

Becky's daughter, Kaley, said, "He's probably right, Mom. Let me take over raising the tomatoes and see if they do better."

"Yeah, Becky," I joked. "Maybe you smashed your green thumb with a hammer and turned it purple."

The subject changed, and we got talking about other things. The summer went by, and I forgot all about our visit about gardening and tomatoes. But in the fall, I invited Becky and her family up for a cookout. We were finishing up roasting hot dogs and marshmallows when the conversation turned to the harvest.

"So, how did your garden turn out this year?" I asked.

"Quite well," Becky said. "Especially the tomatoes."

That was when I remembered our previous conversation.

"So, did Kaley take over the tomatoes like she said?"

Becky nodded. "She did, and they turned out incredibly well."

"Did she talk to them, too?" I asked.

"Yes," Becky said. "I think it's part of our family heritage to talk to our plants."

"So, what did she do differently?" I asked.

"Nothing, really. Same water, same weeding, and same manure. The only difference was what she said to them. She said I was killing them with kindness, and that needed to change."

"What did your daughter say to them?" I asked.

"She said, 'You tomatoes better get your act together and produce lots of fruit, or I'm pulling you out by your roots.' Boy, did they produce!"

The Red Rose

Lewis had fought through World War II in the Pacific. He had seen many of his friends die, and he had himself been wounded. So, when he was assigned as a guard at the war crimes trials in Japan, hatred burned in his heart for those he felt had been the cause of this destructive war.

In his work at the trial, he did not associate too much with the Japanese people, and Lewis was happy about that. He wanted nothing to do with them. And as he did his guard duty day after day, he had lots of time to think about the war, and his hatred increased.

But one little Japanese lady bothered him the most. Whenever she saw Americans, she would offer them a solitary red rose. She especially took notice of Lewis and would single him out for her simple offering. He would reject her gift, as did all other Americans. She seemed hurt by this, but still, each day, she bowed and offered it again.

When the trials ended, and Lewis was released from the military, the hatred still burned in him. He went to his ecclesiastical leader, the bishop, and asked if there was anything he could do to get the hatred out of his heart. The bishop suggested that Lewis serve God in some way, perhaps as a missionary.

"Serving other people tends to remove hatred from your heart," the bishop said.

"But where should I serve?" Lewis asked.

"Why don't you fill out the necessary papers and make yourself available to go anywhere, then leave it in the Lord's hands? Those who issue the calls pray diligently for direction."

Lewis thought a long time about it, and he eventually decided to do as the bishop recommended. He filled out the papers and waited for the envelope carrying his assignment.

He was excited the day it came. His family gathered around, and when he opened the envelope and read the paper inside, the shock he felt was overwhelming. Tokyo, Japan was where he was called to serve. He would be helping the Japanese people recover from the devastation of the war.

Lewis felt the anger and hatred well up in him. He almost refused the call. But when the bishop said, "Perhaps the Lord knows you need to confront the anger in your heart," Lewis decided to go.

There was some basic language training, and then Lewis was off to Japan. He was partnered with a much more experienced young man who knew how to speak Japanese. The two men worked in a little rural community, helping people who had lost almost everything. The people had much of their goods and food taken for the war effort. Many had lost sons and husbands. Lewis began to see these people no longer as the enemy and the cause of the war but as a people who were reluctantly forced to bear the atrocities of it, just as he and his friends had.

As Lewis's two years of service were coming to a close, he realized his heart had been changing. He loved these people and realized that most of them were no different than he was. They did not want war. They wanted to live their lives and raise their families in peace.

Lewis's final assignment was in Tokyo. He had only been there a short time when he ran into the lady from years earlier who had offered him the rose. She recognized him and brought him the rose. It was now dry and in a small envelope. She offered it to him, and this time he accepted it. She told him she was a widow, and her only child, her son, had come up missing in the war. But when the war ended, she learned her son was a U.S. prisoner of war.

"They took good care of him," she said. "And when the war ended, they let him come home to me. I had nothing to offer in gratitude but this rose. Yet, no one would accept it."

Lewis met the woman's son, a young Japanese man who was his own age. The young man was missing both an arm and a leg. He struggled to do the most menial things. When the young man learned that Lewis had also fought in the war, the young man said, "It is usually those who do not suffer the consequences of war who start it, while they who want it the least bear the greatest burdens of it."

Lewis knew that was true, and that understanding, along with love and a rose, changed his heart forever.

The Unusual Date

Joe, my roommate, and his fiancée, Rochelle, came into our apartment. Rochelle came into the kitchen where I was. "Daris, would you be willing to go out with my sister?" she asked.

"Is she going to school here?"

"No," Rochelle replied, "but she is coming with my parents to visit me. I just thought it would be nice if she had a date so she could feel comfortable going to the big concert on Friday with my parents and Joe and me."

"Sure," I said. "I'd be happy to go with her."

"When they get here tomorrow, I'll bring her over to meet you," Rochelle said.

Rochelle went back to be with Joe, and I went back to my studies. The next day, I was busy with classes, homework, and wrestling. I had forgotten about meeting Rochelle's sister by the time I got back to the apartment.

Another roommate, David, stopped me as I came in the door. "Hey, Daris, could you possibly do dishes for me tonight? I've got a big date. I will do them for you on your turn."

"Sure," I said. "I don't have anything but studying tonight. I'll get started right away."

David thanked me and left. I filled one sink with wash water, soap, and dishes. I filled the other sink with rinse water. I rolled up my sleeves and had been busy working for a while when I heard Rochelle's voice.

"Can I come in?"

"Sure, Rochelle," I replied. "I'm back here in the kitchen. I think I'm the only one here."

Rochelle came walking into the kitchen. Right behind her was a girl who looked a lot like her but was slightly shorter and more athletically built.

Suddenly, I remembered I was supposed to meet Rochelle's sister. I looked down at the front of my clothes, with water on them. I looked at my arms with soap to my elbows. I thought the timing couldn't have been worse.

Rochelle didn't even try to hold back her grin. "Daris, this is my sister, Mauren."

I washed the soap off my hands and arms and dried them. I sheepishly held out my hand. "Nice to meet you."

Mauren didn't shake my hand for a moment. I couldn't tell what the expression on her face was. Was she disgusted, angry, annoyed? I just couldn't tell. But there seemed to be a slight grin behind her austere facade. Just as I was about ready to drop my hand back to my side, Mauren took it in hers. But then she looked me in the eye and squeezed really hard until she let go. Still, she never said anything. Mauren silently kept her frozen stare locked on me as Rochelle and I visited for a little while, then the two girls left.

The next day was the big concert, and Joe had purchased all the tickets. When Joe, Rochelle's father, and I went to meet the ladies, everyone seemed excited except Mauren. As we walked to the concert, I tried to get her to talk by asking her questions about herself. Sometimes, she would answer yes or no, but mostly, she ignored me altogether. After we took our seats, I tried again to engage her in conversation, but she stayed quiet. Finally, just when I was ready to give up, she turned to me with an angry expression on her face and poked me in the chest.

"Look, you. I didn't want to go out with you. That was my sister's idea. But there are two things I hate: men and athletes. And from my sister, I learned you're both. So, I also hate you, so just zip it!"

I knew that as loud as Mauren said it, all the others had to have heard. I glanced at them. Only Joe seemed as shocked as I was. The girls' parents grinned but purposely seem to ignore the outburst and instead talked about the concert. Rochelle kind of grinned and shrugged. That confused me, too. It wasn't like Rochelle to set me up for failure.

For the rest of the concert, I sat in my chair, staring straight ahead, but all I could think of was the questions I had for Rochelle the next time I visited with her.

The Unusual Date

(Continued)

Rochelle, my roommate Joe's fiancée, had asked me to join Joe, her, and her parents as a date for her sister Mauren. But when we got to the concert, Mauren told me she hated men, athletes, and me, because I was both. Neither of us said anything for the rest of the concert, and I hardly dared move, always expecting another outburst from her.

As we walked the ladies home, I suddenly realized Mauren and I were alone. I was so focused on getting her back to Rochelle's apartment quickly that when the others slipped off, I hadn't noticed. I felt awkward as Mauren and I approached the door, but I was determined to be as gentlemanly as possible to the end.

I turned to her and tried to smile. "Mauren, I'm sorry I was not the company you wanted tonight, but I'm glad I got to meet you."

I braced myself, expecting her to yell at me again. But she did something unexpected. She smiled. And then she reached out, squeezed my hand, and thanked me for the date before slipping into the apartment. I stood there in shock.

I walked slowly to my apartment, thinking I would never understand females. I went in and just sat in a chair, feeling too bewildered to go to bed. Eventually, Joe and Rochelle came in.

"Where did you all disappear to?" I asked.

"We decided to take a different route so you two could be alone," Rochelle said. "We wanted Mauren to see you would be a gentleman, even without us there."

"But why did you ask me to go with her in the first place if you knew she'd hate me?"

"She doesn't really hate you," Rochelle said. "She's a super athlete and has only dated arrogant athletes who only had one thing on their minds.

When I talked to her about going with you, and she learned you were a wrestler, she said no. But she finally agreed to at least meet you."

"And that was a disaster, with me up to my elbows in dish soap."

Rochelle laughed. "That's the only reason she agreed to go out with you."

"Well, I guess with what she said, we all know what she truly thought of me and the whole date."

I was happy it was all over.

The next evening, Joe, Rochelle's dad, and I had just eaten dinner when the three ladies showed up at our apartment. Rochelle's mom grabbed her husband's arm, and Rochelle walked over to Joe and grabbed his arm. "We want to take you guys out for dinner," Rochelle said.

We had already eaten way too much, and the shocked looks on the two men's faces were funny, because I knew they didn't dare say no. I sat down at the table to do homework in order to hide my mirth. But I got an even bigger surprise. Mauren put her hand on my shoulder.

"And I would like you to join us, too."

Apparently, no one expected that because the room went silent, and everyone stared at her. I was so stunned I simply nodded. And when Joe and Rochelle's dad regained their composure, they grinned.

We drove to a nice restaurant and had a fun time visiting. The food would have been good if I hadn't been so full that I felt sick. When all three of us guys turned down the banana cream pie, our secret came out, and everyone laughed. We had a good time, and Mauren acted like we were best friends. When I walked her home, and we were alone at the apartment door, I thanked her for the date. She smiled, threw her arms around me, hugged me, then slipped into the apartment. I was more confused than ever.

All six of us had fun together the rest of the week, and when Rochelle's parents and Mauren were leaving, Mauren said she wanted to write to me. Rochelle didn't believe it when I told her and was the one who was surprised when I received a letter only two days later.

"I told Mauren that not all guys were like the few she had dated," Rochelle said. "I'd hoped yours and Joe's examples would show her, but after the first date, I felt I'd failed. I'm glad it was successful after all."

And I was glad for a new, unexpected friend.

Questionable Business Decisions

Anyone who has had an accident and dealt with insurance may have come to wonder about the policy-making of modern companies. We had an experience that left us scratching our heads.

The van we wrecked was not damaged too much, but the fender was bent enough that it pressed against the tire. This left the vehicle undrivable. Because of that, we either needed to have the car fixed immediately, or we needed another vehicle to drive. We first approached the body shop to find out how long it would take to get our car fixed.

"The fix won't take too long," the man at the auto body shop said. "The biggest challenge is getting the part. We can put the part on in just a few hours once we have it. But it usually takes about a week to get it. However, for an extra twenty-five dollars, we can have the part shipped overnight, and we could have the car ready tomorrow."

That sounded reasonable, so Donna, my wife, called our insurance company. She explained to the representative about the van and that we needed something to drive.

"That's not a problem," the insurance rep said. "You have a rider on your insurance for us to pay for a car while your van is getting fixed." He then gave Donna the name of a local car dealer that their company worked with. "Just go to them, they will rent a car to you, and we will pay for it," he said.

Donna and I went together in our pickup to the car dealer so one of us could drive the rental car home. We explained our dilemma to the car dealer. He contacted our insurance company and verified we had insurance for a car rental. He then showed us an almost new car.

"How much does it cost to rent that?" I asked.

"We work out a special deal with the insurance company to be their approved car rental company," he said. "We provide this rental for only thirty-five dollars per day."

"Thirty-five dollars per day?" I questioned. "But the auto body shop said they could fix the car by tomorrow for only twenty-five dollars extra for shipping. Wouldn't it just be cheaper for the insurance company to pay the extra shipping?"

The car dealer laughed. "Good luck with that."

We weren't sure why he said that, but we were positive the insurance company would insist we do the thing that would be least expensive for them. We decided we better call them. We went out and sat in our pickup, and Donna called them. Once she had the insurance representative on the line, she explained the situation. When she finished, she said, "So, if you just want to pay for the overnight shipping, we can get our car fixed tomorrow and won't need to rent a car."

"Hold on," the insurance rep said. "You haven't paid for the expedited shipping rider on your insurance. If you want your car fixed faster, you will have to pay the overnight shipping yourself."

"But if you pay for the rental car for a week, it will cost you two hundred and forty-five dollars," Donna said. "Or you could simply pay the extra shipping, and you would only pay twenty-five dollars."

"The problem as I see it," the insurance rep said, "is that you are asking us to pay for something that you did not put on your policy. If we end up doing that for you, there is no end to the extra things people will ask for. You can either take what your insurance covers, or you can pay the extra yourself."

Donna covered the phone and explained the situation to me. "We might as well do the rental car," I said. "We will get to drive a nice, new car, and we will come out twenty-five dollars ahead."

Donna ended the phone call, and we went back inside the car dealership.

The car dealer smiled. "So, are you ready for the car rental?"

He apparently knew what the insurance company would say.

Donna and I filled out the rental papers, even as we wondered at the logic of some business decisions.

Choosing a Musical Instrument

When I first met my wife, she was a music major and played in a dance band. I was in athletics. My children have tended to follow their mother's interests more than mine. Every one of them is an excellent musician.

To be honest, I do play the harmonica, and I used to play the piano some. I also played the guitar when I was in college. But I try not to mention that to anyone because I seldom play a musical instrument in public. I usually only play my harmonica when we are camping as a family, though I have done a little bit in theatre when there was a desperate need, with an emphasis on desperate.

Despite my lack of musical talent, over the years, due to my wife and children's interests in music, I have associated with quite a few musicians. I often find it interesting to learn how different musicians chose their instruments. One fun story was related to us by a physician who played in a community orchestra with my wife. He played the bassoon.

Not too many people play the bassoon. It is usually not the most used instrument in an orchestra. Due to its unique sound, it often stands out and is sometimes given small solo segments. The physician's first name was Paul, and that's what we knew him by in the orchestra. One of the musicians asked Paul if either the unique sound or the opportunity to solo was the reason he chose to play the bassoon.

He laughed. "No. The reason is a lot more rudimentary than that."

He then told us his story. His parents were a family of musicians. Every member of the family was expected to learn to play the piano and one other instrument of their choice. Paul was somewhat annoyed by this expectation. He preferred to play sports.

None of his friends had such a requirement of instrument practice in their families, and he felt frustrated and shortchanged. When he would see his friends head out to play baseball while he was expected to go home and practice the piano, he was endlessly annoyed. So, when he became proficient enough on the piano that it was his turn to choose a second instrument, he chose the bassoon.

"The whole reason I chose the bassoon was not because I liked it," Paul said. "In fact, I thought it was a strange instrument with an even stranger sound. But I knew it was the one instrument that drove my father crazy. I decided that if he was going to make me practice an instrument, I was going to practice something that annoyed him. I guess, secretly, I thought maybe if it drove him crazy enough, he would decide I could quit.

"But if my dad was anything, he was determined. I think he just covered his ears and gritted his teeth. And the more determined he became to see it through, the more determined I became to drive him crazy. I practiced more and more.

"But something happened that I didn't expect. All the practice to drive my dad crazy started making me a good musician. Without realizing it, I was excelling on the bassoon and ended up winning awards and becoming part of the best orchestras. I was nominated to state competitions and ended up winning first in solo performance, even though solo performances on bassoons are quite unusual."

"I bet your dad is proud of you," someone said.

Paul laughed. "Yes, he is. But he has still made it clear that I'm not playing a solo at his funeral. He is having my sister who plays the harp do it instead.

Shoes

One day, when I was in my mid-teens, I was helping an older lady from our community. Leona was a widow and almost ninety. She lived alone and still took care of herself. There was some yard work that was hard for her to do, so my parents would send me to help her now and then.

One day, when I finished the yard work she needed to have done, she offered me some lemonade. I accepted it gratefully. I wiped the sweat from my face and sat down on her step to enjoy the refreshment. She sat in a lawn chair close to me.

Leona was someone who thought deeply about things, and when she spoke, what she said always seemed wise. This occasion was no different.

"Daris," she said, "do you know what I like to look at when I look at someone?"

I took a sip of lemonade and shook my head.

"I like to look at two things," she said. "I like to look at a person's hands and shoes. And do you know why?"

Again, I shook my head, so she continued. "You can learn a lot about a person by their hands and their shoes. Take you, for instance. I can see that even though you are still a very young man, your hands are brown and calloused from hard outdoor work. Your hands show scratches and scars that indicate the work you do must be quite rough. Many boys your age have hands that don't show that kind of work."

Leona then pointed at my shoes. "I can see that you are wearing thick, heavy work boots. They are the kind with a steel toe. That indicates the work you do is tough, physical work that might entail a little danger."

She chuckled slightly as she continued. "I'm sure you've heard people say not to judge someone until you've walked a mile in their shoes. I say that is a good idea, because you've got a mile head start on them, and you have their shoes."

She smiled at me and finished by saying, "But seriously, the next time you meet someone, why don't you see what their hands and shoes can tell you?"

I noticed that Leona's hands were wrinkled with age, and her shoes were soft, older-person shoes. As I went home, I thought a lot about what she said.

A few days later was our community Fourth-of-July breakfast. As I ate, my mind was drawn to what Leona said, and I started looking at people's shoes. Most of the farm boys in the community had heavy work boots like mine, but many of the young men who lived in town wore softer tennis shoes.

There were ranchers in cowboy boots. There was a banker wearing shiny black dress shoes. There were women in high heels and others in sensible loafers. Some families with little money had shoes that were old and worn. Some shoes were meant to work hard, others were for play, and still, others were for dressy occasions. The more I observed, the more diversity I saw.

As we ate breakfast, the speaker talked about this great country and how it was built by people from every continent and every background coming together in a common desire for freedom. He said our differences made us strong and resilient, and our similarities made us united. I thought about how the differences in who we were could be seen in something as simple as the types of shoes we wear.

It has been many years since Leona talked to me about shoes. She long ago passed from this life, but what she shared with me still lingers in my thoughts. It helps me to consider both the differences and the similarities I share with people I meet. It also reminds me that those differences need not be hurdles to harmony but instead can add variety to friendship.

Most of all, it helps me to consider what it might be like to walk for a time in someone else's shoes.

Chico

My daughter, Elli, was going to a music camp in Sun Valley, Idaho. Donna, my wife, would be spending the week with Elli there because I had to work. Sun Valley is an expensive town, so hotels were beyond our means. That meant they would need to camp.

I towed the tent trailer up there on Sunday and helped them set it up. I connected the water and power for them and did everything I could to make sure they were as comfortable as possible before I headed back home. Before I left, a camper pulled into the spot beside ours. We greeted the new neighbors, an older couple, and became instant friends. Their little dog was friendly and seemed to be very smart.

"What's his name?" Elli asked.

"Chico," our neighbors answered.

I know limited Spanish, but Elli had taken it in school. She interpreted for me. "That means 'boy' in Spanish."

"He's a little male dog," the husband said. "That's why we chose that name."

I had a three-hour drive home, so I left. When I came back in the middle of the week, Elli had to show me some things.

"Watch this, Dad," Elli said. Elli then held out a little food to Chico and said, "*Mendigar*."

Chico sat up with his little paws curled in front of him. Elli gave him the food.

"*Mendigar* means 'beg' in Spanish," Elli told me.

Elli said a lot more words I didn't know, and each time she did, the little dog would respond with an action. Chico would roll over, lay down, or play dead. He even danced on his hind paws.

"He's really smart," Elli said. "And our neighbors told us a funny story about him."

Elli said the neighbors had been vacationing in Mexico when they first saw Chico. The man who owned him had lots of dogs. He trained the dogs and then sold them to tourists. The couple had watched the dogs do all sorts of tricks, and they fell in love with Chico. He was smart and cute.

"He beg, sit, roll, bark, and many other thing," the trainer said in broken English. "You just say word."

The trainer gave them a list of words the dog would obey, then the couple paid the trainer and took the little dog with them. They named the dog Rusty. When they got back into the United States, they decided to test out their new pet's skills.

They tried every word on the list the man had given them, but the little dog just stared at them. The husband grew increasingly frustrated. Finally, he said, "This dog doesn't do anything. Maybe he's not as smart as we thought. We ought to return him and get our money back."

"But we know he does those things," the wife said. "We saw him do them."

They both stared at the list for a moment and then, almost at the same time, they realized the problem. The trainer had struggled speaking English, and they noticed that even though the list contained English words, it was poorly written. They concluded the trainer had probably trained the dog in Spanish, and the list was simply in English for the customer.

They looked up the words in Spanish. "*Sentar*," the husband said, and the little dog sat.

"*Mendigar*," the wife said, and the little dog begged.

Elli told me that some words had more than one Spanish equivalent, and sometimes the couple had to try more than one to get the right word. But eventually, they figured out all the Spanish words.

That was when they decided to change the dog's name to Chico.

"After all," Elli said, "the dog only speaks Spanish."

The Summer Vacation

I knew that Brent had gone on an extended vacation, so when he returned, I asked him how it went.

"Well, I learned some things about myself, and I also learned some things about my family and what not to do," he said.

When I asked him what he meant, he told me the story.

Brent and his wife had a new camper on the back of their pickup. Brent thought it would be wonderful to have their four children in back in the camper while he and his wife were in the front alone. The thought of the children taking care of themselves, and he and his wife being able to talk uninterrupted for an extended amount of time, sounded like a dream come true.

"But there's no window between the front and the back," his wife said. "What if the kids have an emergency. They'll have no way of contacting us."

This was years before cell phones were common, but Brent was good at wiring, and he came up with a brilliant idea. He wired a closed-circuit telephone between the cab and the back of the pickup. A person could pick up the phone and hit any button, and it would ring at the other end. When he finished the wiring, Brent asked his oldest daughter to get in the back to test it. She picked up the phone and hit a button. Everything worked flawlessly.

The day for their vacation arrived, and Brent made sure the children had everything they needed in the back of the pickup. The children climbed in, and Brent and his wife climbed in the front. They happily started down the road, but they hadn't even gone a mile before the phone rang.

Brent's wife answered it, talked briefly, then hung up. "David wanted to try out the phone."

She had barely said it when the phone rang again. It rang twice more. Each child had to try it, even the oldest daughter who had tested it previously.

After each child had a chance to try the phone, Brent thought that would be the end of it, but he was wrong. They hadn't gone many more miles when the phone rang again. Their youngest daughter was in tears.

"David took my doll," she said.

"Well, she's hogging the couch," David yelled in the background.

They pulled over and got that all settled, then continued on their way. But they hadn't even traveled another ten miles before the phone rang again. This ended up being the story for the duration of the day. The phone rang about every ten miles. When they were only about twenty minutes from where they planned to camp for the night, the phone rang again. Brent had had enough. When they stopped to take care of a problem between two of the squabbling children, Brent yanked the phone cord out and disconnected it.

"But how will we know if the children are having an emergency?" Brent's wife asked.

"We'll see fire coming out of the back of the truck!" Brent angrily replied.

The children could see their father was mad, and they promised to behave better, but when Brent climbed back in, he was still too flustered to drive.

"Maybe I should drive, and you should relax," his wife said.

"How am I supposed to relax?" he replied. "If I sit up here, I won't know if something goes wrong with the children. And if I sit in the back, the children will all be sulking because I got mad at them."

"Maybe the children should all ride in the front with me," his wife replied. "It's a crew cab, and they'll all fit. Then you can ride in the back and calm down."

"We ended up traveling that way much of the trip," Brent said. "I learned a lot about family vacations and not wiring phones. But it did end up being one of the most relaxing vacations I have ever had. I'm not sure my wife could say the same, though."

Signs of Climate Change

Donna, my wife, grew up in California, while I grew up in Idaho. The differences in our lives can starkly be seen in how we view the temperature. In the winter, as the temperature in Idaho gets down to zero or below, trying to get Donna to venture outside is next to impossible. In fact, anything below thirty-two degrees pretty much puts the kibosh on her outdoor activity.

On the other hand, when it's cold in the winter, I just bundle up a little more and go out, enjoying the crispness of the air around me. Donna says "crispness" does not even come close to the feelings she has for the cold, but she is too much of a lady to say what she thinks about it.

Turning things around, when summer comes, Donna can go outside and seems to feel quite comfortable in just about everything Idaho throws at us as far as heat. As for me, when the temperature gets above eighty degrees, I sweat so badly I feel like I am a walking sauna.

We have our disagreements about which is worse, too hot or too cold.

"Once it gets cold, it's just painful," she says.

"But in the winter, a person can always add more clothes to keep warm," I told her.

"I have never been able to add enough clothes to stay warm and still be able to move my arms and legs," she replied.

"Well, it's worse in the summer," I replied. "A person can only take off a certain amount without the neighbors complaining."

The discussion about global warming in the news has just made the debate more profound. I claim the weather is getting continually warmer, but she is not as sure, especially in the winter. A friend said that the proper term is not global warming, but climate change. He said in Idaho, it is just another word for "seasons."

With the recent heatwave that has hit the country, the debate over the temperature has only increased in our family. I go out and work for as long as I can, but eventually, I have to come in and cool off. This happens about a half dozen times per day. I also buy lots of watermelon and usually eat at least one each day. The problem with this liquid consumption is it tends to catch up to me in the middle of the night, and I get little sleep.

When I complained to my wife about the heat, which was between eighty and the mid-nineties, she was somewhat skeptical. "I think I would refer to that as really warm, not hot," she said.

There have been two things recently that have backed my point of view. The first is our cockatiel. When we let him out of his cage, he will position himself in front of the window fan when it is on, and he will stay there pretty much all day. The second thing was something we saw as we were driving.

As we went past one house, in front of it was a fountain sprinkler watering the parched lawn. There are many sprinklers going this time of year, so that in and of itself was not uncommon. But what caught my attention was not the sprinkler, but what else was there. Often, a person will see children running and splashing through a sprinkler, but in this one, there was a raven. He stood on the lawn about two feet from the sprinkler, with the droplets of water pouring down over him. He had his eyes half-closed as if he were basking in the coolness of the water rolling off his feathers.

I pointed the bird out to Donna. "See, even that raven thinks it's too hot."

She looked at it, and then grudgingly agreed. "Maybe it is just a bit warm."

Theatre and Friends

I had been helping run the lights for a theatre production in a neighboring community when my wife, Donna, saw a Facebook posting. It was a community events page in one of the sites that she often checks. She saw there was a posting about a musical that was getting close to production and needed some more men.

Donna and I have directed plays in our small rural community in the summer, so we know how hard it is to get men. Many of them are farmers or are in some way connected to agriculture, and there are not enough hours in the day in the summer for the work they need to do. Once, when we were producing *The Music Man*, all the men we asked to play Harold Hill turned us down. They were willing to take a small part but not the lead. I ended up playing the part, along with building the set, helping direct, and doing everything I could on the production. Because of these previous challenges when we have been the directors, Donna suggested that I help answer the post.

"But I am just finishing work on the other musical and was looking forward to some time to myself this summer," I said.

"But just imagine if it were us directing again," she said. "Wouldn't you appreciate having someone come help?"

I had to admit that I would. And having been through that challenge, I finally agreed to help. "But tell the director I am not necessarily looking for time on stage and would be happy with as small of a part as possible."

The director was happy to have me join them and immediately brought me a script. I was not able to attend a lot of practices until the other musical finished, but I worked on my lines and music. I had one song that was particularly hard that I had to sing.

When the first musical finished, and I started going to practices for the new one, I realized how far behind I was. I recorded the songs and my lines and listened to them all day for days while I worked. Finally, I started getting them down and could put my script away. Then the director wanted to add the dance. I couldn't seem to dance and remember what to sing at the same time, and I messed up a lot.

The director recorded us doing the different numbers and posted them to YouTube. "Your assignment," she said to all of us, "is to go home and watch yourselves and see what problems you have."

The next day, she asked if we had done what she requested. I was one of the few who had.

"And what did you learn?" she asked.

"I learned that I really look fat on stage," I said.

She laughed slightly. "But didn't you learn anything about how you're performing the numbers?"

"No," I replied. "I couldn't get past how fat I look."

Well, I finally did learn the numbers and worked hard to perfect them to the best of my ability. But the main thing I gained was a lot of good friends. Unfortunately, in the other production, being in the light booth, almost no one knew me, and I made few friends. Most of the people in the production thought I was a parent of someone in the cast. The few times I tried to visit with others, they would remind me parents weren't supposed to be backstage. When I told them I was the person running the lights, one said, "Oh, are you the one the director yells at?" I had to admit that the only time I heard my name yelled through the auditorium was when something on the lights needed to be fixed.

As the second production came to an end, I realized that the true value of being in something like a musical production is in the good friends and good memories a person makes. Nothing else really matters or is really long-lasting.

Wanting to Help

Wanda loved helping, but she especially loved doing it without people knowing. When a woman had a baby, Wanda would sew a baby quilt, wrap it, and put it on the step of the new parents' home. If someone had surgery, she would make sure to leave some food by their door. She always had a magnificent garden and shared most of it with others who were out of work or, for some other reason, could use the food. She was always looking for some way to help.

One day, the leader of her church congregation called her into his office. "Wanda," he said, "I have always admired your yard and gardens. If you have looked around the church, you probably have noticed that the shrubs are quite overgrown and lackluster in their appearance. I was wondering if you would take on the assignment to spruce them up a bit. I'm not expecting you to do it alone; you can ask others to help, but I would really appreciate it if you could use your expertise to improve the church landscape."

Wanda had always felt she had somewhat of a green thumb and readily agreed. She didn't think she really needed any help, either. She immediately set about trimming and fertilizing the shrubs. Trimmed shrubs don't look good at first, but it wasn't long before they were filling out and were beautiful. She was pleased when she heard people talk about the beautiful changes they were seeing in the church grounds.

Being the person she was, she always wanted to go above and beyond the norm. She looked for other things she could do. She noticed that some of the shrubs were not getting enough water. She checked out the sprinklers and realized the water patterns the sprinklers sprayed were not hitting the shrubs just right. She went to a garden store, and they sold her the parts and tools she needed. Then they taught her how to make the adjustments. She worked until the sprinklers were perfect, and she was soaked.

When she finished that job, she realized there were indoor plants in the church and wondered if they also needed watering. She went in and felt the soil in each plant. The soil was extremely dry. She felt the plants looked okay, but they didn't look near as good as the ones she took care of outside. She took it upon herself to hand-water the indoor plants three times per week.

As the weeks passed, the yards outside grew more beautiful. Wanda felt the plants inside did, too, but she wasn't sure. She kept watering them anyway. Then one day, she heard the church leader discussing the indoor plants with a parishioner.

"You know, I think these plants are looking tired and worn," the church leader said. "Perhaps we should get some new ones."

The parishioner nodded. "I'll haul them away and purchase some replacements."

But when the parishioner went to lift the first plant, he couldn't budge it. "This has got to be the heaviest plastic plant I have ever seen," he said.

Plastic plant? Wanda's heart started to pound. Had she been watering plastic plants? She realized the reason the man couldn't move the plant was because the sand in the plant's pot was full of water—water she had put there.

Wanda confessed what she had done, and it took all three of them to move the plant. When they did, they found the carpet beneath it was wet and mostly rotted away. Wanda felt horrible, but the church leader just smiled at her.

"Wanda, don't worry about it," he said. "The carpets in the church needed replacement, anyway. We'll just move the date up a little."

He kindly looked her in the eye and said, "I would gladly replace the carpet or anything like it a dozen times over if everyone in our congregation tried to help as much as you do."

Wanda smiled. She would continue to help, but she would be more careful not to water plastic plants next time.

Lemonade Stand

One thing I love to do in the summer when I have time is to stop at children's lemonade stands. I do like lemonade, but I think the biggest reason is that I have a fondness for children who have an entrepreneurial spirit, and I want them to succeed. That is why I stopped at one on my way home from work.

There were three children there. The oldest girl was about ten, the next oldest girl was about eight, and the boy was probably six. When I stopped, the children became excited. I don't know how many customers had stopped by that day, but for a country road, it had a fair amount of traffic, though it was definitely no city thoroughfare.

The younger girl came running to me as I climbed out of my van. "Would you like a cup of lemonade?"

I nodded. "In fact, I would like four of them, one for each person living at my home."

At the mention of four cups of lemonade, their excitement grew. She ran back to their little fold-up table to help with the order. As I approached the table, I could see their sign not only said they had lemonade for fifty cents, but they had chocolate chip cookies for the same price.

The oldest girl finished filling the last cup of lemonade and looked up. "Would you like a cookie, too? They're only fifty cents."

The second oldest girl flipped her pigtails back from her face and said, "Or, if you want an even better deal, you can get four for two dollars."

"That's not a better deal," the oldest girl said. "That's still fifty cents per cookie."

"It *is* a better deal," the younger girl retorted. "The person gets more cookies, and we get more money."

I couldn't argue with that.

"Did you make the cookies?" I asked.

The oldest girl shook her head. "Our mother did. She doesn't trust us selling anything we make except the lemonade."

"I'd love a cookie," I replied.

The girl reached under the table and pulled out a plastic tray. When she opened it, there were only crumbs. She gasped and turned to the little boy, who stood by silently with cookie crumbs and chocolate all over his face.

"Ricky," the girl said accusingly, "you ate all the cookies."

"Nuh-uh," he replied. "We sold one."

"Well, you ate all the rest," the girl said.

The oldest girl chimed in. "Ricky, how can we make any money if you eat everything we're trying to sell?"

"But it's almost dinner time," Ricky replied, "and I was hungry."

The mother must have heard the commotion, because she appeared, carrying a baby.

"What's the matter?" she asked.

"Mom, Ricky ate all the cookies," the younger girl replied.

"No, I didn't," Ricky said.

"Well, all but one that we sold," the oldest girl said.

The mother smiled and turned to me. "If you can hang around a minute, I have a nice, hot batch in the oven."

I nodded. "For hot cookies, I can hang around."

She smiled again and went back into the house. I visited with the children, and the two girls extolled the virtues of their mother's cookies.

I laughed. "I'm sure I can take Ricky's word on that, huh, Ricky?"

He smiled an embarrassed smile and nodded.

Soon, the mother reappeared with a nice, warm bunch of cookies as promised. I told the children I would take four. I planned to wrap them in a napkin and be on my way.

"But don't you want to try one first?" the oldest girl said. "A sample is free."

I nodded. "I would like that." I ate a cookie, and the chocolate just melted in my mouth. When I finished it, I said, "I'll take a dozen."

"We sell a lot more when we give samples," the oldest girl said.

I laughed. "I can imagine."

As I paid for the cookies and lemonade, I turned to the mother. "I think you need to go into the cookie business with your children as your sales team."

She laughed. "They're good, aren't they?"

"And so are the cookies," I said. "Thank you."

As I headed on my way, I made a note to stop at that lemonade stand again.

If you enjoyed this book, please leave a review on Amazon at:
https://www.amazon.com/dp/1629860239/

Would you like to see the *Life's Outtakes* column running in your local paper or magazine? Suggest it to the editor. If an editor runs the *Life's Outtakes* column due to your suggestion, we will send you a free autographed book by Daris Howard. Find out more here:

http://www.darishoward.com

Read stories, purchase books, or subscribe to our short story list by going to
http://www.publishinginspiration.com

Daris Howard's Amazon page:
http://amzn.com/e/B004H76UGK

For inspiring plays and books, as well as discounts for booksellers, go to
http://www.publishinginspiration.com

About the Author

Daris Howard, an award-winning author and playwright, grew up on an Idaho farm. He was a state champion athlete, competed in college athletics, and lived for a time in New York.

Daris has worked as a cowboy, as a mechanic, in farming, and in the timber industry. He is now a college professor. He has also been a scoutmaster, having up to eighteen boys in his scout troop at a time. In his wide range of experience, he has associated with many colorful characters who form a basis for his writing. Daris has had plays translated into German and French, and his plays have been performed in many countries around the world. For many years, Daris has written the popular column *Life's Outtakes*, which consists of weekly short stories and is published in various newspapers and magazines in the US and Canada.